ABOUT THE AU

George G. Gilman wa
small village east of Lo
until the age of fifteen.
abandoned all earlier a
a professional writer, w
mystery novel. Wrote short stories and books during
evenings, lunch hours, at weekends, and on the time of
various employers while he worked for an international
newsagency, a film company, a weekly book-trade
magazine and the Royal Air Force.

His first short (love) story was published when he was
sixteen and the first (mystery) novel ten years later. He
has been a full-time writer since 1970, writing mostly
Westerns which have been translated into a dozen
languages and have sold in excess of 15 million copies.
He is married with a dog and lives on the Dorset coast,
which is as far west as he intends to move right now.

*The STEELE series by George G. Gilman
and published by New English Library:*

ROUGH JUSTICE

George G. Gilman

NEW ENGLISH LIBRARY

for:
Peggyann Perry
who is certainly a patch
on all the rest – is at
the top of the tree, in fact!

A New English Library Original Publication, 1985

First NEL Paperback Edition December 1985

NEL Books are published by
New English Library,
Mill Road, Dunton Green,
Sevenoaks, Kent.
Editorial office: 47 Bedford Square, London WC1B 3DP

Typeset by Hewer Text Composition Services, Edinburgh

Printed and bound by Hunt Barnard Ltd, Aylesbury, Bucks

British Library C.I.P.
Gilman, George G.
  Rough Justice.—(Adam Steele; 39)
  Rn: Terry Harknett   I. Title   II. Series
  823′.914[F]   PR6058.A686/

ISBN 0 450 05875 1

1

A clock with a tinkling chime began to sound the hour of high noon as Adam Steele rode past the rough-hewn timber marker that was seared with branding irons to proclaim: *ROSARITA. Pop. Growing Fast.* It was an old and weather-ravaged sign that marked the western limits of what the Virginian thought might be one of the earliest Anglo settlements in the Territory of Arizona. For as it basked in the hot and bright sun of a summer's day it had the look of a long-established community. And, as far as he could tell from gazing down the street that ran arrow-straight for the best part of a mile, it looked like no new buildings had been put up in many years. As he kept his big black stallion moving at the same easy walk off the open trail and onto the street, he was not prepared to reach any conclusions about the derelict state of some of the widely spaced buildings that flanked the broad street.

For a moment or so he reflected upon the undeniable truth that it had been a long time since Rosarita had grown at any rate at all: then, with no great urgency, applied his mind to the search for a reason why the single street was empty of people. Not that it was important for him to know why this should be, since the quartet of horses hitched to the rail outside the Pioneer Saloon and Café showed him the town was not entirely abandoned. And the sixth sense for lurking menace that had saved his hide so many times before caused no stir of apprehension on this occasion as he angled his mount toward the saloon on the south side of the street's western extremity. It was simply that it was better for him to keep his mind occupied with inconsequentials than to let it be blank and so prey to wishes that were likely to be unfulfilled and hopes probably destined to be dashed.

Closer to the saloon he was able to hear the rising and falling tones of men's voices, engaged in desultory talk within the sun-shaded interior of the single-story, timber-built, stoop-fronted place. The clock with the chime that was pleasant to the ear had by then ceased to make its unobtrusive sound from in back of the open window of a frame shack immediately opposite the Pioneer. And for a few seconds the only sound to compete with the voices in the uncomfortable rather than unbearable heat of the new-born afternoon was the lethargic clop of the stallion's hooves as they were set down amid lazily-eddying dust on the hard-packed surface of the street. Until a bell began to toll. Just as Steele reined in his mount and made to swing down from the saddle.

The sound was not startlingly loud, for by the time he heard the first strike it had travelled the entire length of the street. And it should not have been unexpected, for it could well have been another clock starting to sound the midday hour. But as Steele checked his dismount for a moment and peered at the distant church tower, he was sure he knew why the street was deserted. And he completed his easy swing down from the saddle to the ground against the measured tolling of the bell that sounded at the cadence of the death knell.

He did not count the number of the mournful notes that were struck, and coincidentally the final clang reverberated through the still air just as Steele slid the Colt Hartford rifle out of the boot: this after he had hitched his horse to the rail at one end of the line of animals that looked to be working cow ponies. Then, as he moved around the rear ends of the horses and sloped the revolver action rifle to his left shoulder, organ music began to drift down the street from the church. He was up the two steps, in the shade of the stoop roof,

2

when many voices were raised in the singing of an appropriately maudlin hymn.

'Stranger, this don't look like your kinda town,' a man growled sourly as Steele pushed between the bat-wings that creaked on dry hinges.

Steele came to an easy halt on the threshold of the place and eyed the interior and its occupants with cool indifference—like he had never expected to find here what he was seeking and was totally unimpressed with what he had found. While he made his impassive survey, he drawled in a voice that suggested he had ridden directly from Virginia to Arizona Territory: 'No town is, feller.'

It was one of the two men behind the bar counter that ran across the rear wall of the saloon who had spoken the less than welcoming greeting: a short, fat, balding man of fifty or so who was attired like he should have been at the funeral service in an ill-fitting suit, a white shirt and a dark necktie.

'Hell, Pa, ain't no point in you takin' out your bad feelin's on a stranger who ain't done you no wrong! And who's fixin' to put some money into the cash drawer, I figure?'

Steele now saw that the son of the ill-humoured man was not much more than a boy: sixteen years old, he guessed. At six feet he was a head taller than his father. Much less heavily fleshed, like his frame was growing faster than the rest of his body could handle. He had blond hair and a pale complexion marred by angry patches of fresh acne and the pits of old attacks. If his father had ever been handsome it no longer showed on his fleshy and world-wearied face, but the boy had the kind of bone structure that suggested he would be a head turner among the ladies once he was out of adolescence. He was dressed in patched dungarees and a heavily stained shirt, and a Stetson was held between his shoulder blades by the leather thong looped around his neck.

3

'The price of a square meal,' Steele answered to the implied question.

'Beef and beans. Chille it up if you want.'

'Beef and beans will be fine, son. Coffee before and after?'

Irritation that was a match for that which seemed a permanent fixture on the father's face paid a brief visit to the youngster's features. But he was eager to be of service again as he swung around to go through an open doorway in back of the bar counter, and called over his shoulder: 'I'll get right to it.'

'You wanna keep my son thinkin' you're a big man, stranger, don't go callin' him son no more,' the funereal-garbed man growled, and directed some of his rancour toward the four men who were obviously the riders off the horses out front of the Pioneer. 'Nor boy, nor kid, nor young'un nor nothin' else along them lines.' He sucked some saliva up from his throat and spat it expertly out of a corner of his mouth; hit a metal target on his side of the bar counter without shifting his contemptuous gaze from the quartet of cowpunchers who sat at a table midway between the entrance and the rear of the place.

It was one of six tables in the Pioneer, each of them with four attendant chairs. All the other tables looked to have been unused since opening time—were stained but clean of debris and stood on areas of floor spread with undisturbed sawdust. Playing cards were heaped on the centre of the occupied table, but the game had been over long enough for all the stake money to be put away. Each of the cowpunchers had a beer glass in front of him, three of them empty except for heeltaps of foam. The fourth glass had some ash in it, from the cigar of the man who had drunk from it. The cigar smoke was sweetly fragrant but was not strong enough to effectively mask the stale odour of sweat that permeated the atmosphere of the Pioneer.

While he moved to the table in the far corner of

the saloon, Steele was aware of the fact that his own clothing gave off the rancid smells of a long ride through several hot days. But if he was ever less than indifferent to how he smelled or looked after riding a long trail, it was never in such surroundings or amid such company as this. In different circumstances he might be concerned about causing offence: sometimes.

'Don't pay no mind to Dunc, mister,' the cigar-smoking cowpuncher said evenly as Steele sat down: selecting the chair which put his back to the corner and gave him a clear view of the two doors, two windows and everyone in the place. 'He does a lot of barkin', but he ain't never been known to bite.'

'Not like you, I guess?' the man opposite the cigar smoker queried. He had his back to Steele and did not turn to look at the newcomer.

'Buck means you,' another man at the crowded table said, and glanced at the Virginian with scant interest.

'On account,' the fourth man said, as he rasped a fingernail over the stubble on his left cheek, 'that a guy who totes around a fancy rifle like you . . . well, he ain't just your run-of-the-mill dude down on his luck like you might appear to be.'

'If you didn't tote the rifle,' Buck added.

'And if you didn't take the safest seat in the house,' the cigar smoker pointed out.

An out-of-luck dude was precisely what Adam Steele appeared to be—and had in fact been for a long time. Lately though, appearance was deceptive. In his early forties, he mostly looked older because of his hair that had prematurely turned from auburn to grey many years ago. His lean face was time-ravaged and element-burnished, and only in a certain level of light at a particular angle did his features hint at the brand of nondescript handsomeness that had been their stamp during the early, privileged years when he had played to the hilt his part as the over-indulged son of one of the wealthiest plantation owners in Virginia. Since those days, violently ended by the gruelling Civil War, his coal-black eyes had witnessed far more than one man's share of the darker side of human influence on the world: and his compactly built frame had been honed to toughness while his emotions were being squeezed dry.

During the early years of the violent peace that drove him out of the East and into the West after the war was finished, he had sought to cling to whatever he could of what once had been—in the doomed hope that he might one day re-establish some semblance of the lifestyle he had considered by right to be his. But today he was as much wiser as he was older, and the cut and condition of his clothes could no longer be taken at face value in terms of the kind of man he was.

He wore a grey Stetson with a black, tooled leather band. A blue-black city style suit. Spurless riding boots and buckskin gloves were solid black. Beneath the suit jacket was a cream-coloured vest, and he also wore a white shirt with a grey silken kerchief in the vee of the open neck. The entire outfit, with the exception of the skintight gloves, had been stylish when it was new: but every item of his clothing was now old and worn and scuffed. And served a purpose that no longer had anything to do with what a man of good taste—and his tailor—might have in mind when such an outfit was purchased. Mostly his clothes were worn to keep him warm when it was cold, protect him from the heat of the sun on days like today and keep him from being arrested as a pervert in towns such as this. Except for the gloves which he wore out of habit; and the kerchief which sometimes became a weapon.

'See Pa,' the youngster said as he assumed a patronising manner in the doorway behind the bar. 'It's like Ma always said about folks. You didn't oughta try to judge a book by its cover. Just 'cause he looks like a citified guy from how he's dressed don't mean he has——'

'You take care not to burn no more skillets, Pierce!'

his father broke in with a recriminatory scowl at the boy. This after the singing of the dirge in the church down the street had come to an abrupt end and the sizzling of hot fat could be clearly heard from the kitchen in back of where the youngster stood.

Pierce's acned face glowed red with a mixture of embarrassment and anger, but he bit back on the first retort that came to his mind. And managed to achieve a tone of ice cold derision as he countered: 'If I do we can always buy a new skillet. But if a person ain't got what it takes to see no further than the end of his nose where certain kinds of men are concerned, well . . . he's likely to make the kinda mistake that ain't so easy to get over. On account of he could wind up dead.' He swept his suddenly hard-glinting green eyes from his father to Steele to ask: 'Right, mister?' But before the Virginian had time to offer a response, the boy directed his demanding gaze to the other occupied table as he rapped out: 'Ain't I right, Mr Ashton? Mr Lowry? Mr Ritter? Mr Wylie?'

Only the cigar smoker deigned to glance at the youngster. 'To die by mistake must surely be a bad way to go, Pierce,' he granted, then took a final draw against the cigar before he dropped it into his foam-damp glass where it hissed out in a pall of smoke and steam.

'Over in Texas,' Buck put in, 'when I was trail-bossin' a drive of three thousand head of Bar-Seven critters, we had a cook who just couldn't get anythin' right. Grub he served up was always either near to raw or burned to cinders. On account of he didn't pay enough attention to what he was hired on to do. Always daydreamin' about what else he could be doin'.' He suddenly guffawed and changed his tone, looked at the men he was addressing as he concluded: 'Weren't you on that Bar-Seven drive, Rex? No, it was you, Marv. How did we kill that lousy cook? Did we drag him, hang him or just plain shoot his ass off?'

There was some more laughter, and Marv indulged

7

in a bout of thigh slapping as he retorted: 'There was a cook we had on the Lucky Lady spread over to Fort Worth way! He couldn't boil water to make coffee, seemed like! What we did, we filled this real big pot with water and we wedged him into it and we boiled his ass but good!'

'He die from that, Marv?'

'No, Rex, but I guess you could say he came to a painful end!'

Pierce needed again to battle hard against the threat of anger born of humiliation as he listened to the banter. But he chose not to take issue with these men who he admired, even though they were making pointed fun of him. Instead, he snapped his head around to glower at his father. But before he could give snarling voice to his fury, his father warned icily:

'Keep in mind your mother's wish.'

It was enough to defuse his rage in an instant. And he was simply despondent as he swung around to return to the kitchen, from out of which wafted an appetizing aroma of frying meat.

'Can I get you somethin' to drink?' the man behind the bar counter asked of Steele, his antagonism toward the world in general now reduced to resignation.

'Just coffee,' Steele answered as the cowpunchers lowered their voices to a conversational level—continued to talk of the cattle business, unconcerned now with anything or anybody outside of what they were discussing. Or so it seemed: until the bell in the church tower at the far end of the street began to sound the death knell again. This as Marv Ritter began to deal out a solitaire hand of cards, Wylie made to bite the end off another cigar and the saloonkeeper looked ready to emerge from his state of apathy and snap a barbed comment at Steele.

Buck Ashton rose to his feet and broke off what he was saying to change the subject. 'Figure they're about to put him in the hole now, boys. That's the part of the whole funeral service that really gets to me.'

8

Rex Lowry got up from the table and so did Ritter and Wylie after the cards were neatly stacked and the cigar was returned to the pack. This as the man behind the bar counter eased his necktie loose and unfastened his shirt collar.

'See you, Dunc,' Wylie said with a lazy gesture of his hand toward the saloonkeeper.

'Hey, Pierce!' Marv Ritter called. 'Takes a man to go along with bein' kidded!'

'And you did all right!' Rex Lowry added.

'Like. always, Mr Nelson, we're much obliged for your hospitality,' Ashton said evenly, his mannered attitude emphasised by the good-humoured grins worn by the others. Then, with a nod toward Steele, he predicted: 'Food'll be good and there'll be plenty of it, mister. You have a nice stay in Rosarita.'

He led the way toward the batwinged entrance of the Pioneer: and now they were upright and on the move the Virginian was able to confirm his first impressions of the four men. All of them about thirty years old, all close to six feet tall and all solidly built. Ritter was a handsome, blond-haired man of the type that Pierce Nelson would probably become in later years. Rex Lowry had the darkest hair and complexion. Wylie was dark-haired, too. The elements had coloured his skin, but fists that had reshaped his nose so that it pointed off centre to the right had also hit hard enough above his right eye and along his left jawline to leave areas of livid scar tissue. Ashton had eyes like shiny grey pebbles and a mouth that was not shaped for easy smiling. His hair was tightly curled, even where it grew in long sideburns that reached down to the ends of his jawbones.

Just as the mounts hitched to the rail outside were quite obviously cow ponies because of the way they looked and how they were tacked out, so were these men cowpunchers. This seen in everything about them from their battered Stetsons to their work spurs, from

9

the knots in their kerchiefs to the style of their belt buckles, from their bulging arm muscles to their bow legs. And the Colts nestled in the hip holsters of three of the men had heavily dented butt bases. The exception was Ashton, whose handgun looked to be in perfect condition from a great deal of careful attention. It had never been used as a makeshift hammer.

'Something you can do for me, Mr Nelson,' Steele asked after he had completed his unobtrusive survey of the four men who were on their way out of the place.

'That won't mean a red cent in the cash drawer, I bet?' Dunc Nelson growled.

On the point of pushing out through the batwings, the man with the well preserved handgun abruptly halted, and this caused the three behind him to come to an unexpected stop. 'Hey there, is that any way to behave toward a stranger in town?' Ashton rebuked the saloonkeeper. 'Pierce was right about how you shouldn't bawl out everybody just because you're——'

'What d'you wanna know?' Nelson snapped, and the glower directed toward the men at the doorway still had plenty of power behind it when he switched his gaze to the Virginian.

'Where I can find Avery Begley.'

Nelson's anger became confusion that immediately was mixed with some fear and suspicion. This as the four cowpunchers all caught their breath and stiffened with tension. The silence seemed to have a palpable presence that warped time after the final note of the death knell had sounded in the hot, still air of the Arizona afternoon. For there were no longer any noises of any kind from out back in the kitchen.

'Why d'you want to find him, dude?' Wylie said, tenderly fingering the scar tissue on his jawline.

'Between him and me, feller,' Steele replied.

Ashton nodded and said as he pushed between the batwings: 'He's down at the other end of the street, mister.'

'Grateful to you,' the Virginian replied as Wylie and Lowry went out of the Pioneer and Pierce Nelson showed at the doorway behind the bar counter, carrying a tray.

Marv Ritter held back to augment with the trace of a soured smile: 'Way down at the end of the street, if you get my drift. Like almost a mile one way. And six feet the other.'

Steele nodded: 'It's his funeral, I reckon?'

'You got it,' the good-looking blond cowpuncher confirmed. And the mirthless smile was transformed into something approaching a threatening grimace before he went out to where the horses were snorting and scraping at the ground as they eagerly anticipated heading for the open range after the irksome wait at the saloon hitching rail.

'Stranger, you just seen a bunch of sure-fire murderers walkin' free in what used to be a fine and decent town,' Dunc Nelson growled, keeping his voice low as he shrugged out of his suit jacket.

'You better stop from talkin' that way, Pa,' his son warned, but also pitched his voice so that the men getting mounted out front of the place could not hear him. This as he brought the tray laden with a steaming plate and cup to Steele's table. And his father followed him out from behind the bar counter, tying a leather waist apron around his middle as he headed for the debris-littered table vacated by the cowpunchers. 'Mr Begley died from natural causes.'

'Grateful to you,' Steele told the youngster as the food was placed before him and the riders spurred their mounts to an immediate gallop, east along the single street of Rosarita.

As the dust of the sudden start began to drift in under the batwings and Dunc Nelson started to gather up the empty beer glasses, Pierce felt it necessary to emphasise the point to the Virginian.

'Doc Bascomb signed the certificate, legal and

11

bindin' and Sherriff Kyle went right along with what it says. Heart attack was what Mr Begley died from.'

'In a manner of speakin', I can't disagree with that, stranger,' the elder Nelson allowed bitterly as he set the dirty glasses on top of the bar counter. Then he scowled into infinity as he rasped: 'Seein' as how them sonsofbitches work for Lucas *Hart*.'

The youngster eyed Steele anxiously, seeking a reaction to what his father had implied. But when the seated man merely took off his hat and gloves and set these on the seat of a chair against which his rifle leaned, Pierce let out his pent-up breath through teeth exposed in a grin of relief. Then, with what came close to a sneering glance at his father, he asked of the Virginian:

'So you ain't hereabouts to take a hand in no local disagreements, mister?'

Steele speared a piece of meat with his fork, pushed it into his mouth and replied as he chewed with relish: 'Right now there's only one kind of beef that interests me.'

2

Dunc Nelson used the underside of his waist apron to wipe the cowpunchers' table clean of wet rings. Then vented a low-toned curse and fumbled to unfasten the apron tie. Snarled: 'Pierce, you finish up cleanin' the mess left by them no good sonsofbitches you figure are such big men! I'm gonna pay my last respects to Avery!'

He flung the apron on the bar counter alongside the dirty glasses and fixed his son with a challenging scowl as he hurriedly rebuttoned his shirt collar and neatened his necktie.

'Sure, Pa, you do what you want,' the skinny youngster replied as he returned behind the bar counter and began to load the glasses on to the tray. 'Wasn't no reason why you couldn't have gone to the service for Mr Begley.' He gulped nervously when this hardened the scowl directed toward him, and waited until his father had spun around and strode out through the batwings before he added through teeth gritted in anger: 'Not if you weren't such a pigheaded old fart!'

He did not rasp the insult loudly enough for it to carry outside against the competing sounds of the swinging batwings' creaking hinges and the purposeful stomping of his father's booted feet along the stoop. Silence began to enter the saloon from the sun-bright afternoon, but it was kept from being absolute by the sounds of Adam Steele eating the food. A situation with which the Virginian was content: and he was as unconcerned as he looked that Pierce Nelson was having to struggle to keep his anger at the level of a slow burn while he gazed intently into an infinity that

13

offered a more compelling vista than that which his father had briefly seen a few moments earlier.

'I'm comin' up seventeen and he still won't allow me to handle the beer and liquor sales,' the youngster growled suddenly. And continued to stare bitterly at a scene only he could see for several seconds after Steele looked toward him. Then he responded to the impassive expression on the Virginian's face with a sardonic smile, a shake of his head and a sigh as he queried: 'Can you believe that, mister?'

'I've got no reason to doubt you, feller,' Steele told him. 'And neither have I got any inclination to kibitz in any family disputes.'

The young Nelson showed not the slightest physical resemblance to his father. And now proved that he could not spit like him, either—the globule of saliva he directed at the cuspidor behind the bar counter impacted dully on wood. 'Real sorry to be a nuisance to you, mister,' he growled with no sound nor sign of regret. 'You don't want to be troubled with talk while you eat, that's all right. You're the customer and the customer is always right. That's what Ma always used to say. And since she had more brains in her pinky than Pa's got under his skull, I mostly try to do things the way Ma used to. Pardon me for botherin' you again, mister, but you're a stranger hereabouts. Rosarita folks and them from close by know the rules. If you want anythin' stronger than coffee, milk or sarsaparilla to wash down the grub, you'll have to wait until my Pa gets back.'

He went out into the kitchen with the tray of dirty glasses and banged them around a great deal without managing to break any as he further let off the steam of his ill humour with a constant muttering that was incomprehensible by the time it reached the Virginian's ears. But after perhaps a minute of this, its purpose was served and peace reigned throughout the Pioneer: which allowed entry to the muted sounds of distant

14

activity as the business of the town was recommenced after the midday funeral.

Steele was not conscious of being watched as he finished eating, but realized the youngster had probably been observing him because of the timing of his return into the saloon with the tray of clean glasses in one hand and a pot of steaming coffee in the other. He stacked the glasses where they belonged and reminded as he set down the coffee pot on the Virginian's table:

'You said before and after you ate, mister?'

'Right, feller.'

'Somethin' else my Ma was always fussin' about,' the dungaree-clad young man continued in the same toneless voice as he transferred the dirty plate to the tray. 'That was never to leave dirty dishes in front of the customers when they was through eatin'. Same as always to clean off the table soon as the customer left it.'

'Your Ma sounds like she was a fine businesswoman.'

'She was fine in just about every way there is. Too good for this rotten world is what a lot of folks said when she took the fever and died so sudden. And so young. Just thirty she was. Six years ago.'

Pierce Nelson's manner had gradually become more detached as he spoke of his dead mother. But there was no sadness in his voice nor in his green eyes as they apparently saw images from the past displayed upon a patch of the wall to the right of where Steele sat. Then, without a trace of change in his attitude, he asked after a brief pause:

'What kinda rifle is that, mister?'

The Virginian finished refilling his cup with coffee and did a fast double-take at the youngster. And concluded that Pierce Nelson had not been peering into the past at all: that he had been reminiscing about his mother as a side issue while he concentrated on a close up study of the rifle that leaned against the chair to Steele's right.

15

'What I mean is,' the youngster blurted suddenly, as he became aware of the double-take and was perturbed by it, 'is that I ain't never seen one like it before. Most folks hereabouts—them that ain't old-timers and carry rifles outside of the house, I mean—well, they mostly got Winchester repeaters. Them four men that work on the Double-H spread for Mr Hart, that's what they carry.'

'I saw that, feller,' Steele told the boy, who had slowly backed off from the table as he spoke the hurried explanation in the manner of one offering a lame excuse for a wrong deed. 'Saw the Winchesters in the boots on their horses.'

Pierce Nelson backed into the bar counter and came to an abrupt halt. He set down the tray on the top and rubbed the palms of his hands down the sides of his dungarees like they were uncomfortably sweaty. Then he swallowed hard and this time sounded genuinely apologetic as he muttered: 'Gee, mister, I'm really sorry if I'm botherin' you that much.'

For a stretched second Adam Steele continued to be puzzled by the suddenness and the degree of the youngster's fear of him. But then he realised there could be but one reason for such a reaction and he spread across his time-lined and element-stained features the kind of grin that in a lower level of light was boyish. 'Reckon I looked at you like I was getting ready to make you the next chore for the local undertaker, uh?'

The boy gulped again and seemed not to trust the easy grin and light tone of the grey-haired, black-eyed, firm-jawed man seated at the corner table. Then felt confident to respond with a grimace: 'If that coffee's cold, mister, it's on account of that look you gave me.'

Steele allowed the grin to gradually fade as he lifted the rifle and raised it so that he could rest the stock on the seat of the chair beside his hat and the barrel leaned against the back. 'It's sometimes known as a Colt Hartford sporting rifle,' he said, and ran the tips of his

16

fingers over the stock that was fire-scorched and had an inscribed gold plate screwed to it. 'And I reckon my Pa would have used it for sporting purposes if there had been the opportunity. But there never was. He died soon after Abraham Lincoln gave it to him. That's what the inscription on the plate says—that Lincoln made Ben Steele a present of the rifle in appreciation of some service I know nothing about. The fire damage was caused when our house was burned down.'

He interrupted his study of the rifle to first put on his hat and then push his hands into his gloves. This as he eyed the still unsettled youngster levelly as he continued with the explanation. 'It was made sometime between eighteen fifty seven and sixty and it was the last percussion rifle manufactured by Colt. It's been adapted so that it doesn't need caps any more. It weighs nine pounds empty. A little more when it's loaded with six .44 calibre rounds. You've seen it's got a revolver action. It's the only thing my father left me and I don't feel inclined to tell you what else I would have inherited if he hadn't done that favour for Abe Lincoln. It doesn't matter. It does matter a whole lot to me that nobody takes the rifle away from me—and I reckon you must have been looking at it with something more than just curiosity to get me so——'

'Yeah, Mr Steele!' the boy broke in eagerly, nodding his understanding and frowning with the intensity of the emotion the Virginian's revelation had released within him. 'I know how that can be! See, I have this real big interest in guns of all kinds. Gee, I'm real sorry if you figured I had some idea about touchin' your gun without first gettin' your permission. Real sorry to have caused you to get riled with me. I didn't mean to. And it ain't just the guns that interest me, neither. I'm curious about the men that carry guns . . .'

The youngster, his enthusiasm for his subject mounting with each word he spoke, now allowed his voice to falter as he swung his bright-eyed gaze away from

Steele: to join the Virginian in looking at the saloon entrance. The attention of both of them drawn by the sound of a footfall on the stoop and then the creak of hinges as the batwings were eased half open by a man with a shiny silver star pinned to the left side pocket of his shirt.

'I ain't so much curious about that as I am worried by it, son,' the lawman said evenly. And used his right elbow to push one of the batwings wider than the other—so that Steele could see the right hand was fisted around the butt of a Remington revolver which was levelled at him. 'When the said man is a stranger in the town where I'm hired to keep the peace. And the said gun ain't just a run-of-the-mill handgun like so many carry in a holster. Instead is some fancy rifle such as a man with a purpose in mind for it might tote around?'

The Rosarita sheriff was more than forty and might have been closer to fifty—had the kind of faintly-lined, sparsely-fleshed prominently-boned face that may have made him look something between forty and fifty while he was still in his mid-twenties. But his eyes would probably not have been so world wearied back then. Narrow lidded, blue-green eyes that looked as if they never showed surprise at anything anymore. His eyebrows were thick and black and no other hair showed anywhere on the front and sides of his head beneath the brim of the grey Stetson that could have been taken off a store shelf ten minutes previously. The rest of the clothes on his six-foot tall, one-hundred-and-seventy-odd pounds frame had seen a lot of wear: none of it hard. His shirt was grey like the hat and had black piping along all the visible hems—down the front, around the collar and the flaps on the two pockets. His pants were black and so were his spurless boots. Perhaps it was just because he had attended a funeral that everything he wore was freshly laundered or pressed or polished.

'Mr Kyle, this is——'

'Name's Orville Kyle,' the lawman cut in on the youngster's attempted introduction. 'Been Rosarita sheriff these past seven years, unopposed since the first election that voted me into office. Not stupid brave nor gunslinger fast with this sixshooter. Mainly kept trouble out of town by meeting it ready to handle it. Shot nine men in the line of duty elsewhere and here. Not anxious to reach double figures. But I can claim as God is my judge that I haven't lost any sleep about killing a man since the first.'

There was just a hint of a Southern drawl in Kyle's voice and Steele thought that the man needed to consciously work at the sound as a part of his play acting the role of a hick town peace officer pretending to be a better man than such a job demanded.

'Adam Steele, sheriff,' the Virginian replied in his natural accent. 'You sound like you're as good a lawman as Mrs Nelson was a businesswoman.'

'I was tellin' Mr Steele——'

Kyle again interrupted Pierce Nelson's attempt to act as mediator. 'On the subject of business, I hear you had some with Avery Begley?'

The boy exposed his teeth in a sneer and rasped through them: 'Pa!'

'I don't know,' Steele said.

The lawman blinked his narrowed eyes for the first time and it was the only sign he displayed that he was puzzled.

'Buck Ashton and the other boys wouldn't have——'

'Don't know if I would have done any business with Begley,' the Virginian told Kyle, to cut across and ignore what the youngster was saying.

The sheriff took a step across the threshold and allowed the doors on their creaking hinges to flap closed. His eyes shone dully and his lips moved hardly at all as he warned: 'I'm a man who doesn't talk around in circles and doesn't like to waste time figuring out what

19

other men are saying to him. So you do some straight talking, Mr Steele, or you're about to spend some time behind bars dwelling on the errors of your ways.'

The Virginian gave an almost imperceptible nod that drew a matching gesture from Kyle. But the lawman's willingness to listen with equanimity to what Steele had to say gradually faded.

'Tell you this, sheriff. Which amounts to what I intend to do. First pay what I owe for what I've had here?'

He glanced at Pierce Nelson who blurted: 'Buck if Pa didn't serve you a drink.'

'No drink except this,' Steele replied, and finished his second cup of coffee as he rose from the chair, delved a hand into his hip pocket and produced a dollar bill that he placed on the table. Only then returned his impassive gaze to Kyle before he continued: 'Now plan to get my rifle—which next to my life is all I care about in the world—and walk out of this saloon through the doorway you're standing in front of. So I'll be grateful if you'll step aside, sheriff.'

Kyle's stance became more rigid and the sheen in his slitted eyes glowed a little brighter as he listened to the softly but deliberately spoken words. And then his thin lips were almost as unmoving as the hand that grasped the Remington butt as he taunted: 'You gonna count to ten?'

Now just the thumb of his right hand moved and the hammer of the revolver clicked back.

Pierce Nelson swallowed hard and it made a wetly noisy sound.

Steele answered: 'Counts are for fights, sheriff. I reckon we're just sparring.'

The lawman blinked once and reminded: 'Like I told you, ten is the number I could be aiming at.'

The Virginian nodded that he did remember, then reached his right gloved hand for the rifle on the chair. Kyle compressed his lips, angled the revolver away from Steele's chest and squeezed the trigger. The youngster vented a sound that expressed high excitement rather than shock as the crack of the gunshot reverberated within the confines of the small saloon. The report and the boy's vocal response to it masked the thud of the bullet into the timber wall behind Steele's left shoulder. There was an eruption of yelling from along the street.

Steel's right thumb snapped back the Colt Hartford's hammer as his hand fisted around the frame and he swept the rifle smoothly up off the chair: turned it so that it was levelled from his hip. And part of a second later his gloved left hand was tightly gripped to the barrel, to lock the muzzle on target.

'Gee, I ain't never——'

The sheriff had thumbed back his hammer for a second shot as he swung the Remington to aim it again at the man who continued to stand erect behind the table. But he hesitated for a moment and Steele did not. So it was the more powerful explosion of a bullet blasting out of the muzzle of the rifle that cut across Pierce Nelson's frenzied shriek of awed admiration for the fluid speed of the Virginian's move.

The bullet had to travel through the gunsmoke-tainted air for less than twenty feet before it smashed into the curled fingers of Kyle's right hand and on the other side of them made distorting impact with the Remington butt. Shock caused the air to burst out of the sheriff's body, forcing his lips to tear apart. This as the velocity of the shot powered him into a half turn before his blood-gouting hand sprang open so that the revolver flew against one of the batwings and bounced to the sawdust-strewn floor. The bullet that had done the damage, misshapen by the hit, was down there somewhere, too. But it had ricocheted to a secret place. The expanding stain of blood was plainly visible beside Orville Kyle's polished right boot as he faced Steele squarely again, both hands hanging limply at his sides.

He was pale under the sun burnish now and there was no sheen in his blue green eyes that were a little wider than usual. He apparently found it easier to keep a frown of shock or a grimace of pain off his face if he kept his lips slightly open.

While the final wisps of drifting gunsmoke were consumed into invisibility by the warm air of the saloon, just the slow drip of blood against the already crimson-sodden area of sawdust kept the silence from being absolute. For the second shot had also quelled the noise from down the street.

'If I'm lucky, it's because you're not in a killing mood today, I figure?' Kyle said and now that he was less self-possessed his Alabama or Mississippi accent was almost gone.

'Hit where I aimed, sheriff,' the Virginian confirmed as he released his hold on the barrel of the rifle and sloped it to his right shoulder. 'Now aim to do what I said I would.'

He came out from behind the table.

'That was a warning shot I fired at you.' The lawman was looking more shaken by the moment and he obviously knew he was getting close to the point where he was likely to collapse. But he forced himself to remain solidly upright, ignoring the temptation to sit on a chair or even lean back against the doorframe. His tone of voice made what he said a bald statement of fact rather than a recrimination.

'Took heed of it,' Steele replied as he advanced on Kyle. 'A man warns me with one shot that close, it's natural I wouldn't want him to fire at me again.'

There were sounds from outside the Pioneer again. Less frenetically strident than before. But rising steadily in volume as the more inquisitive citizens of Rosarita advanced on the scene of the violence.

'Duncan Nelson was right. A man that totes a fancy rifle around instead of wearing a sixgun . . . he just has to be a fancy shooter.'

22

'I ain't never seen no man shoot that straight that fast!' Pierce Nelson managed to get said at last, as the Virginian came to an easy halt a few feet in front of where the wounded lawman continued to stand before the batwings.

'When I need to fire the rifle I always do my best, sheriff. And my best is pretty damn good. If you had just asked me, I'd have told you that and you wouldn't be leaking blood right now. Reckon you should get the local doc——'

'Man handles a gun as well as you do, he has to be a professional, mister!' Kyle interjected forcefully.

From perhaps a hundred yards away, the saloon-keeper called: 'Orville! Pierce! Are you all right in there?'

The babble of curious talk had subsided and Nelson's voice sounded against just the shuffling of feet on the hard-packed surface of the street.

'The boy's fine!' Kyle shouted, without shifting his dull-eyed, demanding gaze away from the impassive features of Steele.

The Virginian pursed his lips and vented a soft sigh. This as sounds of relief were heard on the street. Then he gave a slight nod and answered the lawman's query. 'Now and again I've been known to hire on for a job where it did me no harm to handle a rifle the way I do, feller. But it was never my intention to hire on for any kind of work in this town.'

Kyle continued to fix the man who had shot him with an unblinking stare—like he was trying to peer beyond the stone-faced mask and into the mind where the uncommunicative expression and the evenly pitched words were being formed. Then, after perhaps three stretched seconds, he asked: 'You didn't come to Rosarita because Avery Begley sent for you?'

'No reason in the world Begley should ever have heard of me.'

Kyle remained tensely rigid in his stance and stare for

23

a second longer. Then his pale face expressed a grimace of pain that was not all physical: as he took a shuffling step to the side and sagged back against the wall. 'God-damnit to hell, I believe you, mister!' he growled as he brought his left hand across the front of his body to help raise his right toward his face.

Steele gave a short nod of acknowledgement and then checked his move to step past the sheriff when Pierce Nelson blurted:

'Maybe Mr Hart hired him, Mr Kyle! Maybe he was here to kill Mr Begley for——'

'The same with Hart as Begley,' the Virginian told Kyle as the latent menace in the way he came to such an abrupt standstill forced the youngster to curtail what he was saying.

The lawman scowled at the tall, skinny, almost quaking figure pressed to the front of the bar counter and told him in a tone as dull as his eyes: 'Best you start to clean up the mess I've made here, boy. Know how your father can't abide the Pioneer being less than spotless.'

Pierce Nelson stomped angrily around to the other side of the bar counter and missed the spittoon with more saliva on his way out to the kitchen. This as Kyle sucked on his wounded hand that was now seeping rather than dripping blood.

'You want me to have the doctor make a saloon call?' Steele asked as he hooked his free hand over one of the batwings and glanced out of the Pioneer to where a group of a dozen or so men came to a halt just beyond the stoop steps.

Kyle directed a stream of blood and spit at the floor and scowled at the pulpy crimson tissue between the first and second knuckles of the two middle fingers. 'What I most want is for you to get on your horse and on your way, mister,' he growled. 'But right now I'm in no shape to insist on anything.'

Steele tipped his hat with his free hand as he moved out between the creaking batwings. And halted on the stoop when Duncan Nelson took a pace out in front of the group of men, mostly in suits and black ties, who were standing on the brightly sunlit street before the saloon. Men in an age group of forty-five to sixty who all looked to be merchants or businessmen rather than manual workers. Discomfited, the Virginian thought, more by what he looked like than by the wearing of such clothing on such a hot day.

'What happened in there?' the saloon-keeper demanded, trying to look beyond Steele and over the tops of the batwings at his back.

'A mistake,' the stranger to town answered evenly as he swung to the side and moved down the steps to go toward where his horse was hitched.

'Orville, it okay for him to take off this way?' one of the group on the street snarled in hard tones as Nelson went up the steps and across the stoop.

'Shit, you been hurt!' the saloon-keeper blurted.

'Like the man told you!' Kyle snapped, and showed himself head and shoulders above the batwings: his voice and the sight of him acting to instantly quell the voicing of anger from the group of men who had been about to advance on the Virginian. 'It was a mistake. And I made it.'

Steele reached across the black stallion to push the rifle into the forward-hung boot. Then unhitched the reins from the rail before he swung smoothly up into the saddle.

'You need my services, Orville?' a wiry little man with the purple-veined nose of a heavy drinker asked. 'I'll have to go bring my bag.'

'What I need first is a drink, Doc,' the lawman said wearily and brought up his hand to suck at the wound some more.

'No hard liquor until I've checked you over, you hear?' Doc Bascomb commanded. Then whirled and hurried diagonally across the street toward a once fine frame house, now fallen into despair, which had his name and the initials of his qualifications on a sign above the porched entrance.

'The hell with what the Doc says, Duncan,' Kyle said sourly as he turned from the batwings. 'Two fingers won't hurt me.' He vented a short, sardonic laugh. 'Two fingers of rye, I mean!' he added and broke out with a longer burst of lighter laughter as all the men started up the steps and across the stoop.

This as the Virginian backed his mount away from the rail and turned him to ask for an easy walk along the street. The sound of the lawman's guffawing had caused Bascomb to halt and peer back at the Pioneer when he was several yards short of his house. There was a confused expression on his round, small-eyed, bulbous-cheeked face. And as he rode past the town doctor, Steele told him:

'Reckon maybe he's gone a little crazy, feller. But one sense he hasn't taken leave of is humour.'

3

The Pioneer was the only commercial enterprise at the eastern end of the single street of Rosarita. The rest of the buildings that Steele rode by along more than half its length were houses that ran the gamut of size and style between the simple single-story shack directly across from the saloon and the once elegant two-floored, many-roomed near mansion in which Bascomb had his surgery.

Here and there a house was in an excellent state of repair. Some even stood behind well tended gardens of lawns and flower borders. He saw just two that were blatantly empty: their windows broken, their doors hanging open and with storm-damaged roof shingles left untended for a year at least.

The schoolhouse in back of a fenced play yard on the south side of the street and a meeting hall across from it marked the point where the business section of Rosarita began. Here the buildings were crowded more closely together and, close up, the alert-eyed Steele could see a few of them were of relatively recent construction. The schoolhouse was one of these. So was the stone-built law office and gaolhouse. The Arizona House Hotel was still not finished: no one was working on the walled but roofless second story and it looked as if the project had been interrupted more than just a few days ago.

There was a general store and a half dozen other stores that stocked the staples of life but few of the luxuries. The town also had a stage depot and telegraph office with a line that came in only along the east trail.

Steele had reason to know why this should be since he had covered a lot of ground to arrive at Rosarita from the west: where the rugged Natanes Plateau was spread far and wide to either side of the arroyo called the Black River. He had seen shadows moving out there as the sun arced across the sky above the cactus and outcrop and sandridge-featured country. And the sign left by snakes and birds and small animals and insects. Once there had been a column of dark smoke at a distance—from the cooking fire of a small band of Apaches or maybe of a lone prospector, he had surmised. But the smoke had dirtied the sky in a direction that was off his route, so he never saw where the fire had been lit.

And he had seen no other evidence of human intrusion on the desolate plateau until he reached the start of the trail that led into town. A trail that had been established by a man, perhaps with a family, who had attempted to farm a piece of land close by a cottonwood grove on the river bank. The attempt was doomed, and since the farmstead had been abandoned, the elements of many changing seasons had ravaged the buildings and the fence lines. To an extent where the traces of somebody's ill-starred dream were now almost as faint as the trail that showed no sign of having been used since the last rain had fallen on it or the last wind had raised dust devils above it.

Steele had reflected only briefly upon the outcome of another man's dream as he rode past the melancholy remains of what might have been. And as he rode slowly down the town street he saw with his mind's eye a fleeting image of the collapsed walls, leaning timbers and rusted pieces of iron. Saw this scene in his memory as his gaze swept his new surroundings and there came unbidden to him the notion that the settlers who had failed out at the end of the west trail might possibly be among the people on the street and in the doorways or behind the curtained windows of the flanking

28

buildings—the citizens of Rosarita who peered back at him with a far deeper interest than he showed in them or their town.

He did not resent their curiosity about him: he could understand it, because after all he was not simply a stranger in a town where these were probably few and far between. Also, he had come to Rosarita from out of the desolate west. Dunc Nelson had spread some intriguing gossip about him and there had been two gunshots from the Pioneer after Sheriff Kyle went into the saloon to check if Nelson had good reason to mistrust the stranger. Nobody from the deputation of men who had gone to find out the reason for the shooting had yet returned to slake the thirst for news. So their curiosity, laced with an undercurrent of fear, was perfectly natural as they watched the man who seemed to be making a survey of their town in a manner that suggested a brand of mild interest just a part of a degree removed from indifference.

'Like for you to hold it right there, stranger!' a woman commanded from the open doorway of the Rosarita Bank that was one of the town's older buildings. It was constructed of stone on the north side of the street, between the more imposing timber-built stage depot and telegraph office and the Hope Livery Stable that was a ramshackle shebang of just about every material that could be used to build with. 'And I'm hoping you'll overlook my bad manners if it turns out you're honest and decent.'

The bank and its neighbours were almost at the extreme eastern end of the street. Beyond them on the north side there was just the town cemetery in which there were a great many untended graves and a few that showed signs of loving care: and one new one. The white-painted timber church was opposite the burial ground. Next to the church was a weed-choked vacant lot and on the other side of this was a corral, a blacksmith's forge and the premises of a feed and seed merchant.

The cemetery was empty of the living and the church, the forge, the feed and seed place and the livery were all as quiet as the graves, and could have been as securely closed as far as a first glance showed. There had been sound and activity beyond the open doorway of the stage depot and telegraph office—before the order with its implication of menace was rasped out of the bank entrance. As he reined his mount to a halt after making the half-turn to head him for the bank, the Virginian thought that the woman whose command he had obeyed was probably the same one who had been softly and tunelessly singing before she growled at him to halt, and did not take any of the harshness out of her tone as she added the request.

Steele slowly raised a hand from the reins to tip his hat, and saw a movement to one side of the double doorway as he answered: 'Even if I carried references, ma'am, I might have changed a lot since I got them.'

She stepped onto the threshold so that the Virginian could see she was close to sixty. Short and fleshy of frame and with a square-shaped, strong-featured and homely face. The solid black of her mourning dress and the hat that was a little askew atop her grey-haired head probably made her wrinkled skin look more pallid that it usually appeared. The pudgy hands in which she held a double barrel shotgun aimed in the general direction of Steele from her left hip were ink stained.

'Now, Ellie, ain't no call for you to act so heavy-handed with the stranger,' a man said placatingly as he moved on to the threshold of the stage and telegraph office. He was of an age with the woman. His build was tall and thin and his hair was not quite so grey, except where it grew as a bushy moustache. He wore a brown suit that was either borrowed or had been made for him when he carried more weight. But he had a black band around his left sleeve and his necktie was also black.

'You attend to your business, Fraser Sorrel, and I'll take care of what concerns me and my Earl!' the woman argued. And threw a glance as angry as her tone toward the man. Then took more time to lengthen the focus of her gaze so that she could peer at something which captured her attention out on the timber- and pasture-flanked trail to the east. But suddenly she snapped her head around to concentrate again on Steele. And was momentarily afraid, until she saw he had not taken advantage of her lapse. 'And some business needs your attention is on its way into town right now!'

'Which proves I wasn't making any lame excuse because I was too scared to go with Earl and Dunc and the rest of them to the Pioneer!' Sorrel countered with a childlike brand of triumph. 'Telegraph said the after-noon stage was ahead of schedule and so she is.'

Rosarita was sited across the dividing line between two kinds of country—the near-barren terrain over which Steele had been riding for three days, and the land green with grass and brush and timber that spread down off the plateau all the way to the eastern foothills of the Continental Divide on the other side of the Mogollon Mountains. So, the horizons east of town were much closer than those to the west and the approaching stage coach was less than a half mile away when it first came into sight, emerging from the blind side of a dense stand of pines.

'Earl's my husband, stranger,' the woman with the shotgun said as Steele shifted his indifferent gaze from the Concord stage which had a heavy load of roof luggage behind the driver and guard, and a six horse team in the traces. 'Guess there wasn't no time for formal introductions down to the saloon after the shooting. Earl Webb and I'm Ellie Webb. He'll likely call me a damn fool and that's surely what I'll feel I am, stranger. But when a body whose eyes aren't so clear sighted as they used to be is left in charge of a bank and

31

she thinks she sees a man who might be up to no good make a bee-line for the bank . . . well, it's better to be safe than sorry, I always did say. And if I'm making a damn fool of myself, I've lived long enough for that to be no new thing.'

'You can say that again,' Sorrel muttered, and swung back into the stage and telegraph office as the rattling and clopping sounds of the rig on the east trail reached through the surrounding tranquillity of the afternoon to be heard in town.

Steele looked back over the length of the street he had ridden and saw it was getting to be more crowded by the moment: and that almost everyone was starting to move toward this end. Both men and women, some with babies or small children in their arms. But the mass advance, which he thought included many of the men who had gone to investigate the shooting at the Pioneer, faltered and came to a halt when the people had drawn close enough to see that Ellie Webb was holding a gun on Steele.

'Well, stranger?' the banker's wife demanded, vexed by his attitude that seemed to stress that he was ignoring her while events at a distance held his interest.

'Reckon it's your move, ma'am,' the Virginian told her evenly as he shifted his gaze back to her again. 'Since it's likely I'll get my head blown off if I make one.'

She looked on the point of snarling a retort to this, but then they were both drawn to peer toward the arched porchway of the church at the base of the tower. This as the cassock-garbed preacher used a pulpit tone to make himself heard above the rising volume of sound from the stage.

'A damn fool is what you're making of yourself, woman!' His voice rang strongly with the accent of his native Ireland. 'If you were not such a vain creature—and the good Lord knows you have little enough reason to be—you would be wearing your spectacles and be able to see your husband and the sheriff and the rest are making their way down here without the slightest haste! Just as this gentleman rode his horse away from the saloon in a similar manner after whatever trouble took place there! Do you not think, woman——'

'Ellie! Ellie! Put that weapon away this instant!' The demand was shouted breathlessly by a city-suited and derby-hatted man who had broken into a run along the street. His footfalls pounding against the street were not audible against the barrage of sound from the stage as it rolled past the town limits marker: and his voice, distorted by strain and exertion, was a lot less clear than the preacher's. But his wife's hearing was better than her sight, for she immediately did as he ordered. To the extent of letting go of the twin barrels of the shotgun with her right hand and allowing the weapon to sag so that its muzzles were aimed at the boardwalk beside the hem of her skirts on the left side. Her lips moved to perhaps mouth a silent oath, but she was looking in no particular direction as this happened and so could have been cursing the world in general or herself for being a fool yet again.

Then, as the Concord rolled into town between the church and the cemetery, the driver hauling on the reins and the brake lever as he yelled at the team, it was as if nothing untoward had happened.

Fraser Sorrel came bustling out of his place of business again, eager to be of service to whoever was riding as paying passengers aboard the stage. The Irish preacher remained on the church porch but watched what was taking place with deep interest. Earl Webb slowed from the run and matched the far from sluggish pace of the recommenced advance of his fellow citizens toward the newly arrived stage. The blacksmith on one side of the street and the liveryman on the other emerged from their places that had previously seemed deserted. And Ellie Webb swung around and went

33

from sight into the bank without another glance at the Virginian who, just for a few seconds as the stage came to a dust-raising halt, was conscious of a ball of ice-cold anger starting to form at the pit of his belly.

During this brief segment of time as he sat the big black stallion on the centre of the street that was now filled with activity and sound from which he was totally disassociated, he felt he had a natural right to experience a deep resentment toward these people he had earlier excused. But then as he dismounted, the impulse to anger was involuntarily suppressed and the easy manner in which he completed his advance on the bank was a true reflection of his state of mind.

'Please, sir, I'd truly appreciate it if you will overlook my wife's behaviour——' Earl Webb began to implore as he came to an anxious halt on the boardwalk out front of the bank doorway. He was of an age with his wife and matched her short and stout frame. He had thinning black hair atop a round, weak-looking face in which his red-rimmed dark eyes seemed too small and his fleshy-lipped mouth was too large. A combination of nervousness and exertion caused sweat to pump freely from his pores, and he had taken off his hat, which he moved frantically around and around in his hands: this action almost camouflaging the fact that he was trembling.

It was the sound of Ellie Webb breaking into tuneless song rather than anything Steele did that caused the uneasy banker to curtail his plea. This as the Virginian tied his reins to one of three rings on a hitching post at the edge of the boardwalk to one side of the bank entrance.

'General opinion seems to be that she's made a fool of herself again, feller,' Steele said evenly as what seemed to be the majority of Rosarita's citizenry gathered into a tight-knit group beside the newly arrived stage. 'And somebody as honest and decent as me just has to make allowances for her.'

Webb did a double-take at Steele, to reassure himself that the stranger was not just speaking rhetorically. Then he bobbed his head in grateful acknowledgement and tried to mask his rekindled anxiety when he saw the Colt Hartford slid out of the boot.

'Like I told you, Earl, it's just his way,' the town's lawman growled as he ambled on by the bank as part of a group that included most of the men who had gone to the Pioneer. The two injured fingers of his right hand were bound together in a still spotlessly white bandage. It was impossible to tell whether his soured expression was caused by the pain of his wounds or the bitterness of his thoughts.

'All right, Ellie,' the banker said wearily as he turned to lead Steele into the bank. 'We have ourselves a customer and I'd say he has to be real desperate to do business if he still wants to do it after the way you got off on the wrong foot with him.'

The public room of the bank was small and spartanly furnished, divided equally into a front and rear section by a counter with two chairs on the customer side and two in back of it. The air was pleasantly cool and this effect was probably emphasised by the whiteness of the ceiling and the walls. There were clean looking rugs on the floor, and the counter and chairs shone from regular polishing. Sitting on one of the chairs behind the counter, Ellie Webb looked as cool and clean and businesslike as her surroundings while she made entries in a ledger and abandoned the musical accompaniment to her work. The shotgun was nowhere to be seen.

'Heard what you said to my Earl out there just now, young man,' the woman said, blotting dry the ink of her last entries as her husband moved to one end of the counter, where he raised a flapped section of the top and kneed open a hinged part of the front to go through. 'A fool I know I can be. And I can't do nothing else but take you on trust until you prove yourself one way or another. Fair enough?'

35

The thickness of the stone walls that served to keep out much of the heat of the afternoon also acted to muffle the sounds of the town that were mostly centred out front of the stage and telegraph office. But these had diminished anyway after the stage had rattled to a halt and the initial calling back and forth of greetings had ended.

'I'll go along with that, ma'am,' the Virginian agreed as he took off his hat and sat on the chair across the counter from the vacant one. But a moment later this was occupied by Earl Webb after the banker had hung his derby on a hat and coat stand beside a closed door in the rear wall.

'I'm deposits and Earl's withdrawals,' the woman said. 'And since this bank doesn't have any connection with any other where you might have an account, it seems your business is likely to be with me.'

'I'm in need of advice,' Steele said.

'In that case, you're exactly where you should be, young man,' Ellie Webb allowed with an emphatic nod. Then she retrieved her pen, dipped it in the inkwell and commenced again to copy details from a sheaf of papers into the ledger.

'Financial advice?' her husband asked doubtfully. And he may have been lacking in self-confidence or merely apprehensive that a man with a rifle across his knees was pretending to be something he was not.

'Maybe. It's my intention to get into the horse-ranching business, Mr Webb. Either by staking a claim to a piece of suitable lands that nobody has title to and starting from scratch; or buying a going concern if I can find what I'm looking for.'

The woman suddenly ceased writing, but did not lift the pen from the page: her mind obviously not on her work.

'Around here?'

'Of course around here, Earl!' Ellie Webb snapped scornfully. 'This isn't no greenhorn just got off the

36

latest wagon train to reach the frontier! Think a young man of the world like him would stop by a one-street town bank to talk business that didn't have——'

Webb cut in, his tone and his expression grim: 'Let me tell you, Mr Steele. There's not an acre of good grazing land for fifty miles to the east of Rosarita that isn't solidly owned. To the west, as I'm sure you've seen for yourself, there isn't even an acre of good grazing land.'

The Virginian nodded. 'So if I decided to settle in this piece of country, that's one of my options gone.'

'Nothing's for sale, either,' the banker said quickly, and just as grimly. 'In terms of land suitable for ranching, that is. There are two empty houses here in town and it's possible Matt Hope may be thinking of selling up and leaving Rosarita . . . that's the liveryman.'

'We can't be sure of that, Earl.'

'I said it was possible he was thinking of——'

'I mean the Begley place is as likely to be up for sale as not now that Avery's dead.'

Webb started a glowering look at his wife, then snapped his attention back at Steele when the Virginian said:

'I heard it was up for sale already. That's the reason I came to Rosarita.'

Footfalls sounded on the boardwalk at the front of the bank, and somebody caught their breath. These sounds clearly heard against the near silence that had descended upon the town a few moments earlier. Then a woman drew the gazes of the Webbs to her and caused Steele to turn in his chair and peer at the crowded doorway when she said:

'Then you heard wrong, my friend. And you've had a wasted journey.'

Steele rose from the chair, rifle in one hand and hat in the other. Earl Webb also got to his feet. The fine-looking, elegantly-dressed woman of forty plus who stood on the threshold of the bank accepted this double show of good manners as nothing more than what was her due. And acknowledged the protocol with an almost queenly inclination of her head. Since she was a female her hat and jacket and skirt and boots looked only slightly odd in her present surroundings because the outfit was of such high quality and fine style. Any woman of Rosarita would have given her eye teeth to look so find on the way to church come Sunday morning. Whereas the two men who escorted her were the kind of jack-a-dandy clotheshorses who would always appear misplaced unless they were affecting their foppish styles and attitudes in the swank setting of a city house or country mansion drawing room. One of them was perhaps ten years older than the woman and the other was perhaps half her age. Both looked ready to spring in front of their charge and protect her if Steele should try to use his rifle aggressively.

'If I heard wrong, it wasn't my mistake, ma'am,' the Virginian answered. 'And I didn't have anywhere else to go.'

She gave another regal inclination of her head as the men who flanked her became less tense. Then she said, with a fleeting smile that came within a hairsbreadth of being salacious: 'I'm most glad to hear it, friend. I do so hate to be a source of disappointment to a man.' She turned and moved on along the boardwalk, having to swing around the younger of her escorts as she instructed: 'Come boys, let's see about the carriage.'

'By the way,' the man in his early twenties hurried to say as he held back for a moment. 'That was my mother, Charlotte Begley. The new owner of the Begley place. She therefore knows of what she speaks.'

'Concerning the property, that is,' the older man added as the other went in the wake of the woman. 'Sometimes the lady does not always think before she speaks on other matters. Without wishing to cause offence, I would suggest that you country people do not set too much store by her sophisticated city ways. Good afternoon.'

Ellie Webb vented a snort of scorn and growled: 'City or country style, when a woman simpers like that and says that kind of remark to a man that's a total stranger to her, it's my belief it's only a matter of dollars and cents that keeps her from being a——'

'Ellie!' the banker chided, shocked. Then asked quickly of Steele as he headed for the door, jerking his hat back on: 'Nothing else we can do for you, Mr Steele?'

'If I like what I see and can swing a deal, I'll need a loan,' the Virginian replied from the threshold.

'I figure you've already seen what you like, young man,' the woman behind the counter said sourly and started in with her work on the ledger again, head bent to show the crown of her black hat as she added in a harsher tone: 'And since you said you came here for some advice, I'll give it you—stay out of the Begley-Hart trouble.'

'Nothing foolish about what Ellie's just told you,' the banker added earnestly as Steele continued to stand in the doorway, surveying the single street that was less crowded and a lot quieter at the eastern end now. 'All we loan is cash money. If you run out of living time, only one who can help you in this town is Jack Cooper.'

'That's the Rosarita undertaker, young man,' Ellie Webb explained.

Steele was aware of Sheriff Kyle standing on the boardwalk before the bank where it ended at the alley across from the stage and telegraph office. This as the Virginian nodded absently as he watched Charlotte Begley sweep disdainfully into Hope's Livery Stable after the elder of her escorts had pushed open the door.

'Looks to me like Steele don't give much of a damn about what you're telling him, Earl, Ellie,' the lawman drawled as he came along the boardwalk.

'I wouldn't say that, feller,' the Virginian countered evenly, with the flicker of a wry smile for the lawman who looked more soured than ever now he had seen who got off the stage. 'Never heard any talk about a loan that didn't have some interest.'

4

Orville Kyle laced the sourness of his expression with sneering scorn as he rasped: 'Jack Cooper can fix your kind up to look either of two ways, Steele. Either grinning at your own last joke. Or looking sick that it backfired on you. Providing, of course, that the way you die left enough of your face for him to work with.'

'Have him bury me with a smile,' said the Virginian. 'Show how happy I was that whoever killed me will be brought to justice. By a lawman who just can't fail—the way he happened to have been everywhere I was all the time I was in town trying to mind my own business.'

'Mr Steele says he heard Avery's place was up for sale, Orville,' Earl Webb supplied.

The sheriff sighed and nodded as he showed an expression that was a strange combination of satisfaction that he had got to the bottom of a problem and discontent with how it had turned out. Then he looked rueful and spoke in the same tone as he came to stand beside the Virginian. 'If you had been as open as that with me, there would have been no need for that trouble down at the saloon.'

Steele gave a slight nod and for a moment it seemed that he was to let this be his only acknowledgement as he looked beyond Kyle—to where the stage driver and the Rosarita blacksmith were taking the travel-wearied team out of the traces and the guard and Fraser Sorrel were carefully unloading the large amount of luggage from the roof of the Concord to the street. Almost all the local citizens had drifted away from this section of

41

the street, some of them clutching letters and packages from the stage's mail pouch. Then the Virginian vented an almost inaudible sigh before he returned his attention to the livery into which the woman of natural airs and graces and her two foppish escorts had gone, and replied:

'I'm not usually this difficult to get along with, sheriff. In normal circumstances, if somebody wants to know my business I might or I might not be willing to talk. Especially if I might just be interested in something that I only heard about. But when somebody threatens me with a gun and tries to scare me into talking. Well, if I'm in a position not to co-operate, that's what I go ahead and do.'

There was a rise in the volume of background noise as the team of six horses which had hauled the stage to town was led across the street and into the corral beside the forge. And, at the same time, a flatbed wagon with two horses in the traces and a cut-under buggy drawn by a single animal were driven out of the alley on the far side of the livery. The younger man was in control of the wagon and the other dudishly attired newcomer to town had the reins of the buggy, Charlotte Begley seated to his right in the shade of the roof.

'All right, I'll allow it was all my fault that we got off on the wrong foot,' Kyle growled. And as the two rigs rented from the livery rattled slowly down the street toward the front of the stage and telegraph office where the horseless and unloaded Concord was parked, the Virginian saw with a sidelong glance that the lawman was watching them with eyes as hard as his tone.

'And got a bad hand out of the deal, sheriff.'

Kyle did not look at Steele and so failed to see the fleeting smile that altered the line of his mouth as he made the response. But he was aware of the black humour while he continued to watch the progress of the wagon and the buggy as he countered through gritted teeth: 'Even if it didn't hurt like hell, I'd still find it hard

42

to laugh, Steele. Because there's too much else that's wrong about today.'

Because of the clop of hooves and the rattle of the turning wheels, the exchange between the two men out front of the bank would not have been heard by Charlotte Begley and her escorts. And so Steele's brief smile was misinterpreted by the couple in the buggy after the wagon had driven on by. The woman made an aristocratic inclination of her head to acknowledge the smile she was certain was directed at her. And the man made the same mistake: but he glowered, perhaps in angry jealousy, at the Virginian. Then the woman, her haughty posture on the buggy seat firmly held, shot a sidelong glance past the scowling driver and executed a broad wink that the set of her lips made sultry. Which caused Ellie Webb to gasp and hiss from the threshold of the bank:

'I knew she'd turn out to be as brazen as they come.'

'How, Ellie, we don't know anything about the woman and——'

'Woman?' the banker's wife cut in on her tentatively protesting husband. 'I'm a woman and you're insulting me by calling that shameless Jezebel one, too! What she is . . . What she is . . . We've all had our own notions of the kind she'd turn out to be and it seems to me more were right than weren't. I'm not about to sully my mouth by calling her what I think she is. But I'll tell you this, Earl Webb. I know we have an ordinance against her kind in this town!'

She slammed the door closed, cutting off what her husband had begun to say in defence of the newly-arrived woman. And none of what she had said had carried beyond the two men out front of the bank, to reach the buggy which had rolled to a halt alongside the flatbed at the rear òf the Concord.

'Used never to be hardly a cross word heard in this town, Steele,' Kyle said sourly as two iron-bound trunks and a half dozen matched leather suitcases were

43

loaded aboard the wagon by the young dude and the stage depot manager. 'Of a serious nature, I mean.'

'If there has to be a town close to where I do my horse ranching, a dull one will be the best kind, feller.'

'Dull it was, I guess. The stage there—comes in from Santa Fe just once every ten days. Its getting here was just about the only event of any consequence that used to happen around here on a regular basis. Outside of Christmas and July Fourth. But they have a whole year between them.'

The luggage was all loaded onto the wagon and the young driver waited until the buggy had started out ahead of him for the open trail before he urged his two-horse team forward—so that he, rather than Charlotte Begley and her driver, was destined to suffer the dust raised by hooves and wheelrims. The sheriff took out a plug of tobacco and bit off a small wad as he watched the departure of the two rigs. Then, as a fresh team of stage horses was led by the blacksmith from the stable out back of his forge, Kyle leaned away from the bank wall and invited:

'I can't say I've got no hard feelings, Steele, but I'll stand you a drink at the Pioneer.'

'Took one shot of hard liquor after my wife died, a long time ago,' the Virginian replied. 'It was a mistake. Before that I hadn't taken a drink since I near drank a cantina dry—and decided that a crack on the head works just as well as a bellyful of hooch if a man wants to forget his troubles. Maybe it's better, because the hangover isn't always so painful.'

'Sometimes liquor is all that can make pain go away,' the lawman countered and raised his bandaged hand, in an ushering gesture that also served to point out that he was referring to physical pain. 'You don't want to drink, okay. Not a man better placed than me to know that it's not easy to have you do something you don't want to. But either you take a walk with me down toward the Pioneer and listen to what I have to say. Or you get on your horse and ride out of Rosarita right now.'

At no time did he raise his voice, but as he neared the climax of the ultimatum the force of his words increased. To the extent that some tobacco juice sprayed out of the corner of his mouth and damp stained his shirt. He cursed and was grim faced as he rubbed the brown saliva into the fabric. And held the expression as he warned the Virginian who eyed him quizzically:

'I know I can't force the issue right here and now, mister.' He allowed his bandaged hand to touch the palm to the butt of his holstered Remington, then lowered it. 'But I'm not against using any tactic I have to so long as I do my duty of maintaining law and order in this town.'

'I believe you, sheriff,' Steele acknowledged, and his coal-black eyes were hard with emotion as dark as their colour as he fixed the lawman with an unblinking gaze and added: 'So you'll understand why I don't intend to walk ahead of you.'

Orville Kyle's sun-burnished and finely lined face expressed a brand of anger that seemed to be in danger of going out of control. And perhaps the neatly dressed man with the polished star on his juice-stained shirt might have plunged into a vicious temper if Adam Steele had held the gaze of contempt for a half second longer. But the sheriff's fury was effectively defused by the way in which the Virginian was suddenly eyeing him with equanimity.

'I never backshot a man in my life, mister.'

'I believe that, too. But I reckon you've never been so frustrated in your life, either?'

Kyle spat on purpose now: directing the stream of dark saliva at the street beyond the edge of the boardwalk as he swung around in front of Steele. Then muttered: 'Gunslingers are never smart or they'd be in some other line of work. Guess you're the exception that proves the rule, Steele.' He halted at the hitching post and untied the reins of the stallion from the ring. Then, as he extended them toward the Virginian, he said in an even tone: 'I'm not claiming to be as smart as you, mister. But from what I've picked up, it seems you plan on getting into some other line of work. You know the choice on offer: you can ride on out of town and go about your business in whatever way you've a mind to, or you can listen to me tell you why you should move on a long way from here before you either hire out your fancy rifle or look for a place to hang it over a mantel-shelf.'

Steele moved forward and accepted the reins. 'Reckon I've got nothing to lose but time.'

'Nobody ever lost anything else from listening to advice, young man,' the homely-featured Mrs Webb said sagaciously as she swung open the door of the bank and stepped out into the sunlight, a shopping basket hung over one forearm. 'And if you don't want to lose any more, just light out and keep going until you come to some place where the name Lucas Hart's never been heard.'

'Get on down to the store, woman!' her husband urged from within the bank.

'Yeah, Ellie,' the lawman augmented as the banker's wife scowled at the wall that hid her from Earl Webb, but quickened her pace to move along the street ahead of Kyle and Steele. 'You attend to what concerns you and I'll take care of the keeping of the peace.'

'He came to the bank asking for advice and he got given it, Orville Kyle!' the bustling woman threw over her fleshy shoulder. 'And he got given it plain and simple in a nutshell.'

A combination of a widening distance and a lowering of her voice to an irate muttering acted to render Ellie Webb's ramblings incomprehensible to the two men trailing her at a more sedate pace. This after they had indifferently caught her drift—that she was berating the male of the species in particular because of the way

46

her husband had bawled her out in private and then public.

'Couple of questions before I open up the can of worms, mister?' the lawman asked in a tone of voice and with an expression that suggested he would not be made angry again if Steele responded negatively.

'I don't have too many raw nerves,' the Virginian answered as he slid the Colt Hartford into the saddle boot.

'Where'd you hear the Begley spread was up for sale?'

'Prescott. From a man in a saloon there who'd heard it from somebody else who heard it in a saloon down in Silver City. My man was a down on his luck drummer who needed the price of a drink. He'd heard the rumour I was looking for a piece of land to set up a stud ranch. I told him he'd be welcome to drop by and collect the price of a drink if something solid came out of what he'd told me.'

Orville Kyle allowed his wafer-thin veneer of easy-going amiability to slip a little when he rasped through clenched teeth: 'You don't have to keep telling me how tough and mean you are, mister. I know it already!'

'Just pointing out, sheriff, that I don't take anything a stranger tells me on trust. Especially when he's telling me what he knows I want to hear. If I'm steered to something that pans out, though, then I'm always ready to return a favour. If that drummer stops by——'

'I guess he figured he was giving you good information, Steele,' the lawman broke in as he led the way further out toward the centre of the street. This as they neared the end of a line of stores with a raised, roofed sidewalk along their fronts. The sidewalk was no good for the Virginian who was leading the big stallion. 'It's the first time I heard it, but I can believe Lucas Hart fixed for the rumour to be spread around the territory. It would be one more way to get on Avery Begley's nerves: have a stream of misguided callers come by his

47

place with offers to buy him out when the place wasn't up for sale. Crazy things like that started to happen to Avery ever since Hart made him a final offer and got turned down. Nothing out and out illegal, if you get my drift . . .'

Steele had sensed an undercurrent of tension in the sun-heated atmosphere of the street from the moment he and Kyle started to amble along it in the wake of the scurrying Ellie Webb. And the feeling that all was not as it seemed on the mundane surface had been intensified when the lawman had flared up with short-lived anger. But all seemed well now and the Virginian was able to rationalise about the false alarm sounded by his sixth sense for impending menace. For was it not natural that a man so recently shot at by another should find it less than easy to sustain a charade of amiability toward the one responsible for his pain and humiliation? And surely it was just as reasonable that Kyle's fellow citizens should be wary of the seemingly friendly relationship that now existed between the sheriff and the stranger?

'There was a whole mess of fence posts shipped in to him,' Orville Kyle was saying. 'Enough to close off a couple of hundred acres. And Avery hadn't ordered them——'

'Hold it, dude!' a young man snarled.

'He's covered, Orville!' Duncan Nelson promised.

'And knows it!' Doc Bascomb confirmed.

Ellie Webb snapped, her voice pitched high: 'You men are crazy to mess with one of his kind!' Then, with more force in her tone: 'You let me go this instant, you hear!'

The youngster in a white waist apron had been the first to step out of the open doorway of Bate's Grocery Store. And Steele had obeyed his command before the saloonkeeper and the doctor moved off the threshold and onto the sidewalk to flank the youngster, who had a rifle aimed at the Virginian from his right shoulder.

The still-suited Nelson and Bascomb levelled revolvers from their hips. The hammers on all three weapons were thumbed back and the face of each man behind the gun expressed a grim resolve to shoot at the slightest provocation.

'I'd have warned you, young man!' the banker's wife assured from within the grocery. 'Except that James Bate was part of the sneaky ambush, and he's been holding me back here like only a husband has a right to lay hands on his——'

'Quieten down that old biddy, Pa!' snarled the tall, broad and handsome twenty-year-old with the Winchester in his rock-steady grip.

This as Steele shifted his cold-eyed gaze from the trio of men on the sidewalk to fix it on the Rosarita sheriff: who had taken two further steps forward and then swung smoothly into an about face that placed him immediately in front of the Virginian at arm's reach.

'I gave you fair warning, mister,' Kyle reminded, rasping the words out through teeth that were gritted in a sneer between drawn back lips. His narrowed, blue-green eyes filled with a dull sheen that revealed the extent of his anticipation of imminent pleasure as he completed: 'Any tactic to do my duty.'

He started to clench and unclench his uninjured left hand. And Steele released his grip on the stallion's reins as he acknowledged:

'I recall you said that, sheriff. And so I reckon——'

A man squealed in pain and a woman bellowed in triumph from deep inside the grocery. Then Orville Kyle launched a punch at Steele as the Virginian concluded: '——it's my own fault I didn't watch out for trouble in store.'

5

'She bit me! The cow bit me, Goddamnit!'

Steele had to take that first blow from the tall and powerfully built lawman, who was too slow and clumsy for effective brawling in a one to one situation. For even as he saw the roundhouse punch aimed at his belly clearly telegraphed, he felt certain that one of the men on the sidewalk still had him dangerously covered. Probably the son of James Bate, whose impatience with his father's inefficiency and anger at Ellie Webb for causing trouble might easily find release in an over-eager firing of the Winchester.

So Steele had to pretend to be taken totally by surprise, and his arms still hung loosely at his sides as Kyle's big fist thudded powerfully into the right side of his lower belly. He expected the punch to hurt and it did, exploding a searing pain that forced a groan to burst out of his mouth ahead of the rush of expelled breath that powered open his lips. He had hoped to stay on his feet, perhaps with his back supported by his horse, as the blow drove him into an ungainly backward stagger. But the brute strength behind the punch—vicious with hate—drained him of the ability to think fast enough to take account of how the opening moves of the brawl were not happening in the way he had envisaged them. He staggered back, sure enough, but the horse did not try to back off from him. The stallion stood stock still, and this had the effect of bouncing the Virginian off the point of his shoulder and breast. And at the critical moment when Steele started suddenly forward, he could summon no strength into his legs—because he could not feel his legs. Was totally disassociated from everything about his physical being save for the agony that flared with fierce intensity to every nerve ending in his torso. He was not even conscious of falling forward until his knees smashed into the hard-packed surface of the street and he was assaulted by pain from a different source.

The relationship of the earth to the sky had changed dramatically and as the edges began to melt into each other he had closed his eyes: afraid that confusion of what was real with what a punished mind might accept as a new brand of reality could signal a plunge into unconsciousness. In the darkness the pain seemed not so harsh, and he was able to concentrate on suppressing the urge to give vocal outlet to it. Time was twisted and stretched, and it would have been easy to imagine he had been locked in hurting darkness for much longer than the few seconds it must have been before he recognised the voice of Orville Kyle yelling at him:

'I bet you never figured no hick town lawman with a bum hand and a bunch of his country bumpkin buddies would outsmart a tough talking, quick on the trigger——'

Steele worked at tightly compressing his lips to trap in his throat another groan as he cracked open his eyes. This as the familiar tones of the overweight and less than beautiful Ellie Webb cut across what the lawman was sneering.

'Quit the crowing and get your dirty work over and done with!'

There was a clear distinction between the rooflines of the flanking buildings and the pale blue sky. A dozen or more figures could be seen in dark silhouette against the sun-bleached street, a long way in back of where the Rosarita sheriff towered over him at much closer quarters. The distant forms were unmoving as they peered toward the scene of the violence: perhaps frozen into immobility by shock—or maybe fascination.

51

The only people the Virginian could see nearby, outside of the lawman, were the Bate boy, the saloon-keeper and the doctor, who continued to stand on the sidewalk in the shade of the roof out front of the grocery store. Their guns were dipped now and they showed expressions that signalled a degree of quiet satisfaction with what was happening. Like they considered they had contributed everything asked of them to the completion of a job that could not have been done better.

'That friggin woman is getting to be a pain in the frigging ass!' Kyle rasped softly, so that only he and Steele heard what he said as he took a half step forward—then swung his trailing leg, bent at the knee.

Because he had been struggling to get his bearings as a part of the exercise to fight the threat of unconsciousness, the Virginian only now realised he was down on his knees. That his pain-assaulted mind had not played a trick on him whereby he was a dwarf and everyone else was a giant. And the anger of humiliation at his attitude in the dust before the vengeance-bent sheriff acted to diminish pain. But it was not a hot anger. His life had been on the line too often, and if he had learned anything in the violent past it was that heated emotions encouraged recklessness.

Kyle's knee, his pants neatly creased, came toward Steele's face. The white-hot fire of pain in Steele's belly was doused by the creation of an ice-cold ball of anger. And a part of a second before the swinging kneecap would have smashed into his jaw, Steele rocked to the left. Brought his left arm up and hooked it so the crook of the elbow went under the bent knee. The right hand of the Virginian streaked to where his kneeling attitude caused the slit in the outer seam of his pants leg to gape at the calf.

Kyle's cry of alarm expanded into a roar of triumph as he felt certain he had beaten Steele's attempt to topple him to the ground. But it had never been the

Virginian's intention to unbalance the lawman. For as his gloved right hand was jerked out from the slit in his pants leg, he halted the sideways motion of his body. But he retained his armlock around the leg of his attacker. And tightened it as his other arm swung upward, hand fisted around the wooden handle of the throwing knife he had drawn from the boot sheath. The double-edged weapon was as effective with a thrust as with a throw and he thrust it now, with a forward handed action—but checked it before the honed point found flesh. And Orville Kyle's victory bellow came to an abrupt end and was followed by a pathetic whimper of fear. This at the same time as he froze, just a moment after he got started on attempting to kick clear of the grip on his leg. He even kept high and wide to the side his fisted left hand that he had been about to thud into Steele's temple. The cause of his enervating terror was the knife blade that was held by a faintly trembling fist against his crotch.

'Sweet Mary, no!' he gasped. He stared with bulging eyes down at Steele as he delivered the plea. But then he swung his head to stare at the men who had backed his play. If there had been an instant of hope in his mind as he looked to them for deliverence, it was immediately dashed. 'Back off!' he commanded huskily.

Steele glanced at the front of the grocery now and saw that all three men had him covered again. But none of them was so rock solid in his stance or aim as before. And all of them were sweating in the shade nearly as much as was Kyle in the glaring heat of the sun as they contemplated firing at Steele and hitting the sheriff or—perhaps worse—blasting lead into the stranger but too late to save Kyle's masculinity.

'You want to hear him tell you that soprano?' Steele snarled, and thought that probably only he knew his teeth were displayed and his eyes were glinting in a grimace of pain rather than a snarl of rage.

'Sweet Mary, do it!' Kyle pressed, and his voice was already made unnaturally high by the turmoil of his emotions.

'Aw, shit!' the son of James Bate snarled. And eased forward the hammer of the Winchester before he bent at the knees so that he was able to place the rifle on the threshold of the store and send it slithering across the floor inside. Nelson and Bascomb, expressing misery rather than anger, put the hammers of their Colts to the safe position before they pushed the revolvers into the waistbands of their pants.

'What now, dude?' the young man wanted to know. And started to smile in quiet satisfaction again as he saw Steele unwrap his left arm from around Kyle's right leg. Then, with his knife hand no longer trembling as it held the blade firmly to the crotch of the terrified lawman, the Virginian eased the Remington out of the holster. And it was only as he hooked his thumb over the hammer of the revolver that he sensed something was wrong—that the kid's scornful grin was not born of bravado, and Kyle's terror was getting greater instead of lessening as the threat of death or horrific injury receded.

Then Steele checked the act of cocking the gun and tasted defeat in his mouth that was dried by pain: this as he did a fast double-take up at the face of the lawman and realised Kyle was not staring awesomely into a middle distance in an attempt to detach himself from his anguish. Instead was gazing toward a source of slender hope from which he did not dare to draw comfort: yet.

The stallion whinnied and scraped a hoof on the street. A swarm of flies, dislodged when the animal shook his head, began to buzz around the head of Steele, briefly attracted by the sticky sweat that was beaded at his every pore. Then a circle of metal was pressed into the flesh at the nape of his neck and although the muzzle of the gun could not have been cold on such a hot day it felt to the Virginian like it was crusted with frost. That did not melt as its freezing effect spread in an instant throughout his entire body and dried the sweat.

'If I have to kill you, stranger, it will be a sad day for me,' the preacher said softly, and his Irish roots were more clearly heard now that he was not using a sermonising tone. 'For a man of God must not take life and I will therefore feel duty bound to renounce the cloth.'

'Holy Mary, tell him to take the knife away from me, Masterson!' Kyle demanded croakily.

'I would ask you to do as the sheriff requests, stranger,' the man behind Steele said in the same almost even tone that held just a hint of the sadness he felt at having to take a hand in the affair. 'For as a citizen of this fine community I will feel duty bound to kill you unless you withdraw your threat to our peace officer.'

The Reverend Masterson applied a little more pressure to the gun and suddenly the muzzle felt red hot: sizzling the short hairs on Steele's neck and causing sweat to break out on every part of his body again.

'I reckon I have to believe the word of a man of God,' the Virginian said as he returned the Remington to the holster.

Then Kyle vented a heartfelt sigh of relief as he lowered his arm to his side at the same pace as Steele withdrew the knife from between his legs. And then there was a flurry of movement on the sidewalk: as Nelson and Bascomb drew and cocked their revolvers and the Bate boy ducked in through the store doorway and re-emerged with the rifle. He aimed it from the hip this time, so that the beam on his face was fully in view.

'Okay, Mr Masterson!' the young man snapped gleefully. 'You did real good. We got him in our sights again now.'

'I'm much obliged to you,' Kyle said and recaptured Steele's impassive-eyed attention away from the gloating Bate and the rather doleful looking older men who

55

flanked him. The sheriff sounded like he had to work hard to beat a compulsion to roar with laughter at his deliverance. And then he did vent an uncontrolled guffaw, and attempted to mask his true reason with a joke. 'Guess I'll have to make a greater effort to attend services in future.'

'The point has been proved, Mr Kyle,' Masterson said solemnly as he withdrew the gun muzzle from Steele's neck. And the Virginian craned his head around to see that the short and stockily built man of fifty or so was now holding the Deringer down at his side, still cocked but aimed negligently at the ground. There was an expression of poignant entreaty on his pale, hollow-cheeked face as he continued: 'If you are truly grateful to me, you will simply make the stranger leave our town and——'

The cassock-clad man abruptly showed dismay as he curtailed the plea. And Steele had no time to snap his head around and see the reason for the sudden change of attitude. He instinctively took a tighter grip on the knife he had never released. But then the knee of Orville Kyle made delayed contact with his head. He was forced to whiplash backwards, and because he was on his knees the base of his spine crashed painfully against the heels of his boots. The side of the jaw where the kneecap had struck hurt so much he was sure the bone had been broken. But then, as he squeezed his eyes closed and was unable to prevent himself toppling over on to his side, all the pain was suddenly concentrated at a single point, and it was so intense he was certain he had reached his time of death. For it was in an area of his chest, left of centre, that the agony was centred. And there flashed into his racing mind a memory of the Nelson father and son talking of the heart attack that killed Avery Begley.

He snapped open his eyes for a final view of the world at the end of a life that had given him such a raw deal for such a long time. And taunted himself for a fool because of the indulgence in self pity. This as he saw in blurred vision the booted foot of Orville Kyle as the sheriff drew it back after delivering the vicious kick. What Steele had thought was a punishment-induced roaring in his ears came to an abrupt end a part of a second after he recognised it as a chorus of voices raised to express a whole range of emotional responses, from glee to disgust.

The Reverend Masterson warned in a voice that came though loud and clear to Steele: 'In the name of God, stop it! You'll kill the man!'

'It was what you were ready to do!' the Bate boy shrieked in high excitement.

'He was a threat then!'

Although Steele's hearing was now impaired as he found he had to fight for his breath, he was sure that he detected agreement with Masterson's point as the consensus of opinion in a new eruption of vocal sounds. Then his pain-misted eyes saw unhurried movement just a few inches in front of where his head rested on the warm surface of the street. Something shaded him from the sun and he blinked rapidly in the hope that he could bring the dangerous world into sharp focus.

'You sure as hell ain't that any more, right?' Orville Kyle queried evenly.

And the Virginian felt the pressure of a gun muzzle against his flesh again. His eyesight was still blurred, but from what he could see and feel and hear he was able to reason what was happening to him. He was curled up on his side on the street, winning his struggle to breathe normally but in danger of blacking out from the pain that was now filling his entire being again. The Rosarita sheriff was hunkered down on his haunches, casting a shadow across his face. Kyle was holding the Remington in his left hand, but he could be confident of firing a fatal shot since he was pressing the muzzle firmly into the flesh below the left ear of his potential victim. Steele was vaguely aware that the trio of men on the sidewalk and the town preacher were no longer the only bystanders close to him. For a crowd had begun to gather in an arc in back of where the sheriff squatted.

Steele flexed the fingers of his right hand and discovered the knife had slipped from his grip. His kerchief, that could be used as an effective weapon on certain occasions, was at present as useless as the Colt Hartford in the boot on his stallion's saddle.

'You know it, feller,' he said and to his own ears his voice sounded like he was speaking in a small, bare room with an echo.

'That is real fine,' the lawman answered slowly and distinctly, his Southern accent stronger than Steele had ever heard it. 'And you should know, mister, that you are under arrest.'

'What the hell for, Orville Kyle?' the familiar voice of Ellie Webb demanded to know from out of the vague background that existed beyond the Virginian's world, which at that time was comprised of himself in pain and the Rosarita sheriff with a gun at his head.

'Disturbing the peace sound good to you, Steele?' the lawman asked evenly.

The Virginian replied grimly: 'It sounds better than rest in it.'

6

Because the passage of time was irrelevant to him, Adam Steele took no trouble to try to keep track of it as he lay on his back on the narrow cot in one of the two cells that adjoined the Rosarita law office.

He had been brought there between Nelson and Bascomb who had put up their Colts while Kyle walked behind him, Remington aimed at a midway point of his spine. This after he had accepted without comment the assistance of the doleful Masterson in getting to his feet: when he had discovered that he could remain upright and then move unaided. That he hurt worse standing up than he had curled up in the dust of the street was something else that registered: but the pain was not bad enough to warn that bones had been broken or damage had been done to vital organs. During the short, unhurried walk from out front of the Bate Grocery Store to the law office and gaolhouse he was unable to see anything clearly because the glaring brightness of the mid-afternoon sun combined with the effects of the beating to keep his eyes in soft focus—whether he was looking at the ground a yard ahead or trying to peer into the distant west beyond the end of the street. But he could sense something about the townspeople who watched his ignominious progress toward the lock-up: some were feeling as satisfied with what had happened as were his escorts and the Bate boy, while others were sympathetic to his plight and disgusted at how it was brought about. The son of the grocery store owner had put into triumphant words how one faction felt and Ellie Webb had argued against him in angry contempt on behalf of the other side. This before Kyle snarled at the both of them to cut it out and signalled the start of the walk along the street, through the dispersing group of bystanders who mostly only watched the tight-knit quartet of men. Although some did pass low-toned comments that raspingly allied them with Kyle or ranged them against him.

Little time was wasted inside the law office. With a minimum of talk, Steele was searched for further concealed weapons—an apprehensive Doc Bascomb patting him down while the sheriff continued to keep him covered with the Remington. While this process was attended to, Dunc Nelson complied with Kyle's request that he should take the key from a desk drawer and open one of the cell doors. Then, nothing taken from him as a result of the search, the Virginian was ordered into the open cell with a gesture of the Remington. It was the lawman who clanged the door closed, turned the key in the lock and removed it.

Apart from the town doctor's sweating nervousness as he tensely ran his trembling hands over Steele's clothes, the sheriff and his helpers had been un-emotionally efficient after they had brought their prisoner in off the street. For which Steele was impassively grateful. Also, he appreciated the coolness of the atmosphere and the less brilliant level of sunlight within the stone-walled building. Most welcome of all was the cot which had a solid timber base but with a blanket-draped straw-filled mattress and pillow on top. It was not until he had stretched out on the cot that he became aware that somebody had jammed his hat on his head. And he tipped it forward over his face, to further reduce the intensity of light assaulting his eyes.

There he had lain, indulging in the luxury of resting his body as he waited patiently for the pains of the beating to diminish. Resting, too, his mind, that as yet was not filled with angry memories of what a fool he had been or notions of how he might take his revenge against those who were responsible for his present situation.

At first he was vaguely aware of talk in low tones as the three men engaged in what sounded like desultory conversation on the other side of the wall to which the cot was pushed. He made no attempt to eavesdrop, and heard the rising and falling drone of the voices as just a part of the background noise of the town that filtered into the lock-up area of the building through the two glassless, barred embrasures that pierced the wall on the street side. The townspeople went about their business quietly, and for most of the time they all contributed to a body of sound that was perhaps more conducive to restorative rest than utter silence would have been.

Once a saddle horse clopped by and now and then a rig rattled and creaked along the street. Because he was not attempting to monitor passing time, Steele had no idea how long it was after he was locked in the cell that the saloonkeeper and the doctor left the law office. For a few seconds or perhaps a number of minutes he felt weary, but thought that the aches in his legs and torso would not allow his mind the comfort of sleep. Then a mid-toned bell began to clang, and as he responded to it with a jolt and folded his back up off the cot, he knew he had drifted into sleep.

His hat fell off his face as he sat up, and the instant he saw his surroundings clearly he recalled in detail all that had happened to him until he lowered himself onto this cot and waited for the curative powers of time to work on him. He swung his legs off the cot more cautiously than he had raised his back. And as he decided that the first self-diagnosis about the seriousness of his injuries had been correct, he thought he identified the reason for the urgently ringing handbell. When it stopped, the thudding of running feet and the excited shouting of children confirmed his guess. School was out.

He retrieved his hat from the floor and set it on the cot as he rose to his feet. His knees hurt more than the base of his stomach, the left side of his chest and the bruised area of his left jaw and cheek. But his legs made no threat of collapsing beneath him as he paced back and forth within the confining distance of a dozen feet between the barred door and window. On the other side of the door was a short lobby that gave access to this cell and the one separated from it by a line of floor to ceiling bars—in the same way that the doors were set in a line of vertical bars strengthened by a horizontal band at a midway point. A one-piece wooden door with a three-inch diameter hole at eye level would open into the lock-up area from the law office. The rear and side walls were of unfaced stone beneath a ceiling of stout timber beams. The empty cell was as spartanly furnished as the one in which Steele did his pacing to get the blood circulating through his mistreated body again—just the cot with the minimum of bedding and a bucket. The place looked and smelled neat and clean, and Steele sensed that neither cell had been occupied for a long time before he was brought here.

When he had walked much of the ache out of his legs, he stood at the narrow window for half a minute or so, flexing his muscles and gently massaging his chest where Orville Kyle had delivered the damaging blow with his boot. Immediately across the street from his viewpoint was the unfinished hotel. To the right of this was a small house behind a neat, fenced garden and next to this was the school. All the students had now gone from Steele's field of vision. But he did see the middle-aged and frail-looking schoolma'am as she made her way from the school to the house, carrying a stack of books. She paused in the garden to stoop and uproot a weed. Then, as she made to bend down again better to breathe in the fragrance of a rose, she sensed the Virginian watching her. Just for a moment she met his incurious gaze with a frown of fear: before she whirled and hurried to go into the sanctuary of the house.

The woman's reaction to him kindled the threat of anger within the Virginian as he contrasted his initial impressions of the town of Rosarita with his current opinions. But then he shifted his gaze to survey as much of the street as he could see in the other direction. And he was able to suppress the futile emotion as he saw what was taking place out front of the row of stores to the east of the roofless hotel. Here there was a barbering parlour, a meat market and a bakery with a tree-shaded length of sidewalk along the front. The Reverend Masterson sat in a rocking chair in the tree shade outside the barber's, and seemed to be gazing everywhere but at the man at the cell window—until the familiar form of Ellie Webb emerged from the doorway of the bakery and said something to attract his attention before she stepped down off the sidewalk and started across the street with a resolute gait. He then almost sprang up from the rocker and hurried to join her, the both of them constantly switching their gazes between Steele and the facade of the law office a few yards to his left. Masterson, who was empty handed, looked nervous. The woman expressed the same brand of determination as was evident in her stride as she carefully carried a shopping basket and made sure it did not swing overmuch.

'I think it important——' the stockily built preacher began.

'He's here to tell you how sorry he is, young man!' the woman, who matched the preacher in height but carried more weight, broke in; her voice almost strident in contrast with the soft Irish accents of the man. 'I'm not against sentiment, but first things first. A man has to eat and drink and when he's had his fill of——'

63

It was her turn to be interrupted now, by the sheriff who flung open his office door with a forceful sound that signalled his mood to the unsighted Steele before Kyle said in a snarling tone: 'It's real nice of you people to stop by with comfort and sustenance for the fast gun who shot your peace officer and then near gelded him!'

'Mr Kyle, I——' The preacher hooked a forefinger inside his clerical collar and moved it from side to side, like he felt he was being choked.

'From what I heard and saw with my own eyes, wasn't nothing happened to you that you didn't invite by your damn fool——' The more angry Ellie Webb got, the plainer she appeared to be. And her features were as ugly as her mood as she again cut in on Masterson.

'Nice for me, too!' Kyle broke in, moderating his own tone to one of cunning. 'Because I've got business out of town and I need to deputise a guard for the prisoner. You can consider yourself duly deputised, Mr Masterson. And you, Mrs Webb, have saved me the trouble of having to see he gets fed. I really do appreciate your help and co-operation.'

'But I can't!' the preacher protested.

'Of course you damn well can!' the woman snapped. 'You was eager enough to take a hand in this rotten business earlier on this afternoon. Go attend to your out of town business, Orville Kyle. And you can ride easy knowing Mr Steele's being well taken care of.'

The lawman vented a grunt of acknowledgement that implied he was not so sure of this. Then he came out of the law office doorway so that he could be seen by Steele, and see him. He was carrying a Winchester rifle that looked to be as well cared for as his revolver. He also carried a sheepskin coat of the kind Steele favoured and was in process of putting on his hat—atop a head that truly was totally hairless except for his bushy black eyebrows. 'Plan to turn you loose in the morning, mister,' he said, his blue-green eyes as impassive as were the Virginian's coal-black ones. 'If I'm back by morning, that is. Should be.'

'Where are you going, Mr Kyle?' Masterson was anxious to know.

'You know my policy of law and order enforcement, Reverend. Head off trouble before it has a chance to happen. Intend to go have a talk with those highfalutin' city folks that came in on the stage. Then maybe swing out to visit with Lucas Hart. Figure as my duly appointed deputy you got the right to know that, Masterson.'

'What if something crops up that I can't——'

'Locked up the way he is, Steele won't cause you any problems,' Kyle growled, checking the act of swinging away from the law office. 'What other kind of trouble ever comes to this town?' He shrugged his broad shoulders. 'You know the brand of community spirit we have in Rosarita. Help won't be slow in coming.'

'I have a question, feller,' the Virginian said, and drew a sound of impatience from Ellie Webb as the lawman again delayed his departure. 'My rifle and knife, and my horse and everything on him: all my belongings are safe?'

Kyle scowled and spat and in his saliva there was just a faint stain of his last chew of tobacco. 'Nobody steals in Rosarita, mister. Either off their neighbours or off of strangers. Your mount's being well taken care of by Matt Hope at the livery. All your tack and the rest of your gear are in the office. Everything'll be returned to you in the same state or better than when it was confiscated. Afternoon, Mrs Webb, Masterson.'

He tipped his hat and strode out of Steele's angle of vision, headed east: presumably to get his own horse from the livery.

'Good afternoon, Orville Kyle,' the woman called after him coldly, then muttered softly but forcefully, 'and good riddance!'

'What the sheriff said about your belongings is sure to be true, Mr Steele,' the preacher assured, eager to please. 'There will be no trouble about——'

'Oh, attend to your duties as a deputy, whatever they are!' the impatient woman urged and bustled out of Steele's sight to enter the office.

Masterson looked helplessly around, but saw nothing or nobody on the street who he felt could assist him in his predicament. Then he peered up at the sky that was shading to a softer tint of blue as the less harshly bright sun slid beyond the midway point in its afternoon arc down the south western dome. If he offered up a silent prayer in the short time he held his head tilted back his expression of misery suggested he felt there was little hope his plea would be answered.

'Least you're better qualified than the average deputy, feller,' Steele told him evenly.

'I am qualified only to preach the word of Almighty God, sir!' Masterson countered, and seemed to be caught between irritability and apprehension. 'Why, even that ridiculously tiny pistol I pointed at you to prevent bloodshed was not loaded!'

The Virginian experienced a flare of anger as he heard this admission, but killed it after his eyes had glittered for just a part of a second. Then, smiling with his mouth as he heard the door from the office to the lock-up open behind him, he told the preacher:

'The usual run of lawmen can only guard what they see. You can take care of me body and soul.'

'At the best of times, sir, I am not amused by humour that makes fun of religion and the religious.' He spoke the retort as he went from Steele's sight into the law office: and emphasised his depth of feeling with a slam of the door that was as angry as the manner in which Kyle had wrenched it open.

Ellie Webb drew the Virginian to turn away from the window as she announced sourly through the bars at

66

the other end of the cell: 'You don't exactly go out of your way to have folks like you, young man.'

He looked at her earnestly as he allowed: 'Reckon I don't, ma'am.' Then he showed her the grin that used to be boyish as he added: 'But nothing good comes easy.'

7

The wife of the Rosarita banker asked Adam Steele: 'Are you at all interested in what I think of you, young man?'

'You've got a small audience but it's a captive one, ma'am,' he told her. 'And although I'd rather be somewhere else doing something else . . .' He shrugged. 'I'll be happier listening to you in here than I was when you were holding that double-barrel shotgun on me, Mrs Webb.'

She showed the ghost of a smile as she shook her head ruefully and then sighed: 'It was quite a reception you got here in town, wasn't it?'

'Last time I had so many guns aimed at me on one day was probably at Shiloh.'

It was a few minutes after the woman had entered the lock-up and the preacher had reluctantly assumed his responsibilities as a deputy in the law office. Athough Steele had said he was not hungry, Ellie Webb had unloaded her basket and pushed food into the cell through a horizontal slit in the bars of the door. There was a half loaf of bread, a hunk of cheese and two still warm boiled eggs. She had called through the open doorway to the Reverend Masterson that he should light Kyle's stove and make coffee. The preacher had done some muttering of complaint, but then there were sounds that indicated he was doing as he had been asked.

'I think you're a victim of circumstances,' Mrs Webb announced. And stepped into the second cell, where she sat on the cot—on the pillow so that she was able to rest her back against the front wall of the lock-up and swing her feet off the floor. Thus was she able to look through the dividing wall of bars into the Virginian's cell without having to crane her neck.

'Reckon we're all that,' he replied as he sat on his cot and rested his back to the wall between the lock-up and the law office.

'Can't argue with that. But I guess you know what I mean in particular? Some folk's circumstances are a whole lot worse than other folks.'

Masterson stepped into the connecting doorway and was morose rather than aggrieved as he qualified: 'There are some, it seems to me, who can be said to go out of their way to invite trouble.'

'Hey, the poor guy's locked in the hoosegow through no real fault of his own!' the woman accused and her eyes directed a scowl toward the man in the doorway. 'Be a whole lot more punishment than he deserves if he has to be forced to listen to one of your moralising sermons, Michael Masterson.'

'And some that just can't seem to help stirring up the dust when other people are around, feller,' Steele allowed, his tone and expression detached from the here and now as he gently massaged the bruised area on the left side of his face.

'Nothing worthwhile comes easy to us in life, sir. All of us who seek to achieve our laudable aims must strive to take into account that we are not islands in a vast sea of——'

'Orville Kyle—or anybody else for that matter—tell you about the trouble between Avery Begley and Lucas Hart?' the woman cut in. And there was scorn on the turn toward anger in her dark eyes as she glared briefly at the preacher. Then, after he had responded to the look with an expression that seemed totally devoid of christian thought, she peered through the open door of the cell at the rear wall of the lock-up: and saw, on the stonework, images that threatened to touch off the fuse of her rage.

'Just that it killed Begley,' Steele answered. And shot a glance at the preacher that was impassively commanding.

'I'll attend to making the coffee,' Masterson said with resignation. And added as he turned to re-enter the law office: 'But I'll be able to hear what you say to him, Ellie.'

'Nothing that won't be the truth,' she answered the one man, but looked at the other with an expression of sincerity replacing the earlier anger on her plain face.

'Why, ma'am?' Steele asked as a first trace of the aroma of brewing coffee found its way into the lock-up on a cool draught of evening air. 'The food was more than enough.'

'Because it would be pointless not to tell . . .' She faltered and then vented a small sound of annoyance with herself. 'Oh, I think you mean why should I be here fixing to jaw your ear off?' She paused, but to frame an answer to her own question rather than to wait for his confirmation. Then: 'Pride, I suppose. In myself and my husband. In the town and most of the folks that live hereabouts. You seen us at our worst and I figure it's important to set the record straight as to why Rosarita people been acting up the way they have. So, same as the food, I guess. Hoping you'll know we're as sorry as I say we are—but just saying sorry to a man don't make his lumps hurt any less, does it?'

'No, Mrs Webb.'

'Nor does it' she gave him an up-from-under look. '——persuade a certain kind of man that there ought to be room for him to forget and forgive?'

In the law office the Reverend Michael Masterson had been moving about and rattling tin cups together. Abruptly he was silently still. And it almost seemed as if the whole town was waiting just as anxiously to hear the Virginian's reply to Ellie Webb's question—for not a sound filtered in off the street through the barred windows of the lock-up.

70

'I've always been willing to forgive my enemies, ma'am,' Steele said.

'That's good to hear.'

'Soon as they're dead.'

The preacher dropped a cup and the banker's wife caught her breath.

'I don't always feel the need to kill them.' He ran the fingertips of a gloved hand along the aching length of his jawline again. Then invited: 'Not prepared to tell you right now whether or not I'm open to being talked into allowing you to keep your local lawman in one piece.'

Masterson vented a low, strangled cry and Ellie Webb swallowed hard before she was able to entreat:

'But you'll listen, young man?'

'Whatever you have to say will have to rest easier in my mind than what's already in there, Mrs Webb.'

'Good.' She nodded with an emphatic motion, then had to pause to organise her own thought process. Eventually launched into the explanation with far less confidence than she had shown when she first came to the lock-up. 'Avery Begley was well liked and highly respected in this town. Guess you must have figured that out for yourself: from how the entire town, almost, went to the burial. You came in off the west trail and you probably saw the old Begley place out by the Black River cottonwood grove. Still some sign of it left, I'm sure?'

'Enough to show there was a farmstead there once.'

'That was where Avery first settled hereabouts. At a time Rosarita was no more than a couple of stores, a church that's since fallen down, a shack that was Duncan Nelson's first saloon and our bank. Off to the east there was a whole lot of other dirt farms and Avery should've staked a claim over there with them. But he always said he'd come out from New York City to find some space. He wasn't a man that disliked other folks—just the kind who only liked to see them when

71

he wanted to. Had a pretty young wife who never said she didn't agree with his line of thinking. And there were twin little ones not old enough to have any opinions.'

The preacher had brought two tin cups of coffee into the lock-up, and by his manner showed that it was not his intention to intervene: this as he set down one of the cups on a spot where Steele could reach through the bars for it and then went into the other cell to hand the second to Ellie Webb. He went back into the law office and then re-emerged to stand in the doorway with his own cup of coffee as the woman continued:

'The Begley family had three good years out at Cottonwood Farm. Same as other settlers on the better land to the east of town. And Rosarita started to grow. Then both the Begley little ones took sick with the typhus. Died within hours of each other. Their mother grieved for a week before she drowned herself in the river that went past the place. Avery was working in the fields when she killed herself. He buried her alongside the grave where they'd both buried the babies. Then he hitched his horse to the buckboard and headed out across the badlands to the west.'

'I was there and watched him,' the preacher said sorrowfully, holding his cup in both hands and peering down into its steaming contents. 'He'd asked me out there to perform the burial service. There were just the two of us and after he thanked me and told me I was to sell everything of value on the place and put the proceeds toward the building of the new church, he left. I tried to talk him out of leaving. At least he should not go out into the wilderness, I told him. If he did not die of hunger or thirst, at that time there were many bands of hostile Apaches roaming the Natanes Plateau. But it was as if I were making entreaties to a deaf mute. And when I attempted to restrain him by physical force he knocked me to the ground as if I were a mere boy.'

'That was almost twenty years ago, young man,' Ellie

Webb said, eager now to take up her version of the account again. 'And for the next two years we all thought he must have perished. But then he came back to Rosarita. A rich man by our standards. And I should know, since he deposited his cash in Earl's bank. But he didn't keep it sitting there for very long. Started to buy up the places east of town. Offered good prices to the folks ready and willing to sell. Later on better still to those who needed persuading. Took him fifteen years before he got all the land he wanted. Fifty thousand acres it says on all the title papers he held. All of it the single spread, of course. All the old places and their fences knocked down. Except for the one he first bought. He just moved in there and started to live in it the way it always had been before he bought it. And he farmed a few fields, ran some hogs and a few head of beef cattle. Kind of let the rest of his property go back to the way nature intended it.'

'A lot of people thought he must be crazy,' Masterson went on while Ellie Webb took time to sip her coffee. 'But many more of us realised he was simply leading the style of life that had always attracted him. Without a wife and family any longer, of course. But he had his little farm isolated from neighbours he did not have to see unless by his own choice. Encircled by land that could not be settled because he owned it. Perhaps he was indeed a little unhinged. The degree of tragedy he had endured must leave a mark of some kind upon a man.'

'But he never did a solitary thing to harm anyone, Steele,' the woman put in, her tone insistent. And she set down her empty cup on the floor and rose from the cot. To peer out through the barred window as the gathering murk of approaching evening suppressed the final harsh glare of the afternoon sunlight: overlaying the yellow brightness with the dull red of a dying fire. 'Just lived his life the way he wanted—and had the money to afford. Kept himself to himself almost all the

73

time, but was always the perfect gentleman in all his dealings when he had occasion to come to Rosarita. Were a few people hereabout who held he was selfish to keep all that land to himself and do hardly anything with it. Held that if it was sectioned off like it once was all the different families that worked it would have made Rosarita more prosperous. But most of us figure we haven't done so badly for a one-street town at the end of the stage route and a telegraph line. Still a few scattered places worked by folks that didn't sell to Avery or that he never planned to buy. Them folks need what we can supply here in town. Same as the men who work for Lucas Hart.'

She paused, but not for effect. Instead to do a double-take at something that had caught her attention on the street. She pushed her unattractive face closer to the bars of the window and vented an unladylike grunt just before her husband called lightly:

'So this is where you've got to, Ellie. That'll teach you to interfere with law business.'

'I'm here of my own free will!' she countered irately. 'Trying to undo some of the harm Orville Kyle and some others I could mention did——'

'Pardon me, dear,' he interrupted. 'But you obviously have some other poor man who has to listen to you right now. So I guess I can be excused to take a quiet drink at the Pioneer while——'

'Go to hell, Earl Webb!' she snapped and spun away from the window.

Her husband chuckled as he went on by the lock-up toward the saloon at the far end of the street.

The preacher made a sound of rebuke that might have been drawn by the woman's mild curse or Earl Webb's dismissive attitude toward his wife. Then took up the account of Rosarita's recent trouble. 'Mr Lucas Hart was ranching in this area back when the town was first established, Mr Steele. A few miles to the east on the Mogollon Rim, let it be said. At the start we

74

townspeople saw little of him: and his men came to Rosarita only very occasionally. There was never any trouble. And when he became more successful and needed to expand the Double-H Ranch, he spread to the east and the north and the south. Until there was no more suitable cattle country in those directions. But he still wanted to enlarge his land holdings, and so the only way to come was westward. And then it was the turn of Avery Begley to be offered a fair price for his place. But he told Hart he had no intention of selling; and after this, I'm afraid the . . . the trouble began.' His voice dropped and he shook his head sadly. 'The trouble that led to that poor, tragic, helpless . . .'

'That killed the crazy sonofabitch!' Ellie Webb said into the morose silence that the preacher had left as he ran out of soft-spoken words. And in the fast-gathering gloom of evening her voice probably sounded more harsh than it was because of its stark contrast with that of Masterson. 'First some fence lines got knocked down. Then grass fires flared up for no good reason. A coyote got trapped in Avery's chicken run one night, would you believe? And that rumour you heard got started when a whole mess of For Sale signs was nailed to trees on his property. A fishing pool on his place suddenly got poisoned. For more than a year that kind of lousy thing happened to Avery, young man. And Orville Kyle wasn't ever able to find out a damn thing that showed that Lucas Hart was behind what was happening.'

'Now, Ellie, the sheriff did try to investi——'

'Did I say he didn't?' the woman snapped at the preacher. 'And why don't you throw some light on the situation we have here, Michael Masterson?'

'I'm sorry?'

'Light a lamp. Sun's near set and as a deputy sheriff you can't keep a proper eye on the prisoner if you can't see him.'

'Deputy sheriff indeed,' the preacher murmured as

he swung out of the doorway to do as she suggested. 'I think you are more fitting to hold such a position than I.'

The woman resumed her frowning survey of the street as the fragrance of woodsmoke permeated with the aroma of cooking food began to waft in through the barred windows. And said as light from the newly-lit lamp spilled into the lock-up from the law office: 'You're not a man to ask many questions, Mr Steele?'

The Virginian had taken off his gloves, and as he broke open one of the hardboiled eggs he told her: 'Ma'am, you were there at the bank when I asked what I wanted to know.'

'Does that answer mean you've got no interest in what Michael Masterson and me are telling you?'

'Could be you're leaving nothing unsaid,' he answered. And then rekindled her eagerness to go on when he probed: 'You were getting around to saying that the Rosarita lawman did his best, Mrs Webb?'

She nodded as the preacher returned—content to leave the lamp in the law office to shed meagre light through the doorway, for he carried his refilled coffee cup in one hand and the pot in the other. He quietly set the pot down on the floor where Steele could reach through the bars and replenish his cup. And this was done, the men nodding in acknowledgement to each other, as the woman responded to the Virginian's prompting.

'He's good at his job, which is sheriff of a hick town. Lucas Hart is smart and has money to hire on smart help when the need arises. Fact is, everyone knew what was happening—who was doing what to who—but if you want a town run on a tight law and order rein, all the rules got to be abided by. Without proof of guilt, wasn't nothing Orville Kyle could do.' She sighed and shook her head. 'Then poor Avery died and wasn't no other way to look at it but as an accident from how it happened. There was a stampede of Double-H cattle

76

that had the whole herd going hell for leather on to the Begley place. Hart's men claimed they couldn't stop the critters because they were so spooked up. Did manage to swing them away from Avery's house at the last minute. Avery allowed that himself. While he lay dying after some of Hart's men brought him to town. Seems he took a hand in heading the stampede away and the strain was too much for his ticker. He died in Doc Bascomb's house no more than an hour or so after he was carried in there.'

'And how the town felt about the way he died may be judged from the size of the congregation at the funeral service,' the preacher added in a tone of sadness that was a match for that in Ellie Webb's voice when she spoke of the recent death. 'But I'd be telling less than the truth if I told you I thought the size of the attendance was due entirely because of the high regard in which the deceased had been held.'

'Damn right!' the woman cut in, and her near venomous tone was directed out through the window along with a reproachful scowl. 'Almost all them that were there went there out of a feeling of guilt. Because all they ever did while that poor sonofabitch was being driven to his grave by that land-grabbing Lucas Hart was to throw up their hands and make sounds of pity.'

'But what else could——'

'I know, I know!' she cut in on the man attempting to excuse the townspeople. 'And I know, as well—same as you do—that Orville Kyle feels more shame than anyone about not being able to lift a finger to help Avery.'

She had turned from the window to stare at Masterson. Now swung out of the cell and halted at the barred door to glare through at Steele. But she was able to moderate the expression in her dark, weak-sighted eyes to a brand of entreaty before she concluded: 'And I know that's why he acted the way he did toward you, young man. He figured you for the kind of trouble he could

77

handle. But under normal . . . if we hadn't buried poor Avery just a short time before, the sheriff would never have been so brutal.'

She gazed at him for stretched seconds after her plea was ended. And he could see that she needed to struggle hard to keep a grimace of mounting anger off her plain face while he chewed on some bread and cheese. But he swallowed the food and was able to respond to the woman before her rage exploded.

'I'm grateful for the trouble you went to to bring me supper, Mrs Webb.'

'Nothing else?'

'And your company.'

'But you still mean to cause trouble because of what has——'

'If I've ever caused trouble it was never because I meant to. Sometimes I set out to end it.'

She seemed about to press the point. But then she snorted and snapped: 'You really are the most infuriating man!'

'Stubborn and self-opinionated, too,' Masterson augmented as Ellie Webb gestured for him to step aside so she could leave the lock-up.

'Can't deny it, I reckon,' the Virginian allowed. 'Amazing how much Avery Begley and I had in common.'

'And remember what happened to him, young man!' the woman said ominously as she pushed between the preacher and the door jamb. Concluded from the law office as she strode angrily across it: 'He's dead!'

Steele waited for the door to slam behind her before he washed down a final piece of egg and bread with a swallow of coffee and drawled: 'Reckon I'll worry some about that until I'm turned loose from here.'

'I assure you, sir, you have no need to be concerned on that score,' the preacher assured. 'The sheriff truly does take his duty seriously and holds the law in high regard. When I intervened in this afternoon's violence it was as much to save him from himself as to prevent you from taking further punishment. As that woman told you, Mr Kyle was not——'

'Yeah, I'm convinced, feller. The Rosarita peace officer is one of the finest in the land. And I bet he's got a good supply of the elephant powder, too.'

Steele was starting to feel painfully stiff from sitting in one position for so long. And he eased tentatively to his feet with a grimace as Masterson asked, confused:

'Elephant powder?'

'You spread it over the streets of a town and elephants never come near,' Steele growled as he began to pace the short length of the cell again.

'But there are no ele . . . Oh, I see. It's some kind of joke.' But he was ready to be angry rather than amused.

And the Virginian's features were impassive rather than grinning in the wake of the grimace as he replied: 'More an allegory than a joke, I reckon. Maybe there are no elephants because of the powder? The same way that maybe Kyle's such a hotshot peace officer because nobody ever disturbs the——'

'No, that is not strictly true, Mr Steele,' Masterson cut in earnestly on the slowly pacing man in the cell. 'The sheriff once tracked down and had to shoot three men who robbed the Webb's bank. And he has on several occasions been required to deal with trouble among drunken customers at Mr Nelson's Pioneer Saloon. Mostly that was caused by hands off the Double-H Ranch on pay nights.'

Steele decided there was little point in taking so much trouble to keep his muscles from getting set at this early stage of his incarceration: and so he abandoned the exercise and lowered himself on to the cot again, at a point that allowed him to swing his legs up and to rest back with his head on the pillow.

'Yeah, I met four of Hart's cowpunchers in the Pioneer. Liquored up, I reckon they could raise some

79

hell.' He lifted his head off the pillow to peer along the length of his body and between the bars at the uncertain preacher to add: 'And I'm not trying to make a joke this time.'

'Yes, I saw Ashton and the others ride into town and then leave after the funeral,' Masterson countered in a manner that suggested he was eager to put his relationship with Steele on a man-to-man, equal basis that ignored the bars between them. 'And I agree with the consensus as to why they were in town.'

He paused and there was a near-palpable query hovering in the silence of the meagrely-lit lock-up. The Virginian, his head back on the pillow and his brooding gaze now directed up at the ceiling, confirmed his interest with the assumption:

'Charlotte Begley and the two men with her were expected to reach Rosarita in time for the funeral?'

'Nothing was certain, Mr Steele. So much time had elapsed. You see, in the final few minutes of his tragic life, Avery Begley knew the end was near. And he requested that after he was gone a letter should be written to Charlotte and Dale Begley at an address in San Francisco. To tell them what had befallen him and that he bequeathed to them the land for which he had died. And he also asked that his funeral be delayed for two weeks to give his family an opportunity to attend.'

'No strings attached to the legacy, feller?'

'None. He said they should be told in the letter that they might do as they wished with their inheritance. His requests were adhered to, and it was even decided to use the telegraph rather than the mail to give the surviving members of his family a slender chance of reaching Rosarita in time for the funeral. But we held out little hope of the message drawing a response, Mr Steele. For this was the first that anybody had ever heard of him having relatives. And as far as we were aware he had not had any contact with anyone outside of this community since he returned here after the two-year absence that followed the tragedy at Cotton-wood Farm.'

He stooped to retrieve the coffee pot and the cup that Steele had used, before he concluded: 'Those four men from the Double-H have been in and out of town for the past several days. For no other reason than the obvious one, it appears. And I can but assume that the distraction of the funeral, perhaps allied with your arrival, caused them to overlook the fact that the stage was due to reach town today.'

'But maybe Kyle will save the Double-H boys another trip to Rosarita to find out they left too early, uh?'

Masterson sighed deeply. 'He did say he might go out to see Lucas Hart, didn't he? We can but hope and pray that whatever he has in mind to do will result in a peaceful end to this tragic business.'

'If praying can do any good, you're better qualified to swing something than I am, feller,' the Virginian drawled. 'Best you count me out of that "we" stuff.'

The preacher sighed again, less intensely, and answered: 'I can assure you in all sincerity of one thing, Mr Steele. If I honestly considered that your way of dealing with this matter was superior to the method my calling forces me to employ, I would unlock this cell door and you could go about your business with my blessing.'

'I'm grateful for the thought, reverend,' the Virginian murmured. 'Especially since blessings are something I'm a little short on right now. But, right now, I don't count anyway.'

8

Stretched out on the cot in a cell of the Rosarita lock-up
that provided greater comfort than a lot of other places
where Steele had spent a great many nights, his physical
hurting diminished for as long as he did not move. And
since there was no prospect of immediate freedom with
an opportunity to salve his emotional hurts, he found it
easy not to dwell on what they were and how he might
negate them when the proper time came. Thus resigned
to his present circumstances it would have been a simple
matter to drift off into an untroubled sleep had his mind
and body needed such a degree of rest. For outside of
his being everything about his immediate surroundings
was peacefully conducive to sleep.

The low light combined the glow from the lamp in
the law office and that of the moon in the southern sky.
The temperature was pleasantly regulated between the
night air from the windows and the stove warmth that
wafted through the doorway. In this gently stirring
atmosphere there hovered the fragrances of coffee and
cooking meat and woodsmoke that served to emphasise
the Virginian's feeling of being well fed because they
reached him as a subtle background to the clean fresh-
ness of the night instead of filling it. Just as the sounds
that came into the lock-up were unobtrusive—the turning of a book's pages or the creak of a chair seat from
the law office as the Reverend Michael Masterson tried
to stay comfortable and to fill his time as a deputy
usefully; the infrequent crying of an infant that was
made to be strangely melodic by distance; the footfalls
and occasional snatch of low talk from people who

moved on the street—and never came close enough to the barred windows to give the Virginian pause for thought; and the general mixture of a hum and a buzz that provides an audible backdrop to any community during its most peaceful periods of the daily round.

Briefly as he indulged himself in this ambience of relative luxury, Steele allowed the forefront of his mind to be occupied by random recollections of what he had seen of Rosarita and the notions that his impressions of the town had triggered. No town was his kind, as he told Duncan Nelson. But a man who ran a horse ranch could not be entirely self-sufficient and this single street community at the end of a trail and a telegraph line to nowhere seemed to be capable of supplying him with everything he would be likely to need.

What he certainly would not need if he were to put down roots on a piece of land outside of this town was trouble with the local lawman and a rich and powerful neighbouring rancher. So, if he were able to buy the Begley spread—and he first had to see if it was suitable for his purpose and then talk business with the city-style new owners—it seemed like there were some men to bring around to his way of thinking before he turned his attention to horseflesh. And as for every other citizen of Rosarita . . . well, he would have so little contact with them he had no need to cultivate their respect or even their goodwill.

'. . . boy is just a loud mouthed braggart!' Ellie Webb was saying in a contemptuous tone, her voice coming into the lock-up from off the street. 'But James Bate, Earl—I tell you he was holding me against him so that I could feel——'

'All right, Ellie,' her husband broke in on her diatribe, sounding weary. And his voice trailed away as the two of them went on by the cell windows without pause. 'But him and me are both sixty years old. You expect me to challenge him to a . . .'

Adam Steele discovered that the woman's righteous

anger sparked a mild irritation at himself that he had allowed his mind to probe so far into a future that as yet did not have the faintest trace of a foundation outside of his own wish that it would exist. Then, a few moments later as the sights and sounds and smells of the town reverted to what they had been before the interruption, the Virginian felt himself become as involuntarily calm as his surroundings.

'Whatever was to be, would be' seemed like a defeatist philosophy; but it was, he was prepared to allow to himself tonight, one that his life had more often proved valid than not. Today—and for days, weeks, months and perhaps more than one or two years in his recent past—he had been attempting to show to his own benefit that it was reasonable to expect that he could live a paraphrase of the tenet: that something of what a man wanted to be could be. So long as he was single-minded enough to fight for what he wanted without let-up.

Infuriatingly stubborn and self-opinionated was how the banker's wife and the preacher had combined to give their view of him. And, in all honesty, he could not refute that he was this for most of the time as he rode from one failed prospect of making his dream come true toward the next opportunity where he might get lucky. So, he reflected as he became conscious of every aspect of his surroundings getting even more luxuriously comfortable, maybe he should not take himself to task so much when he found himself giving in to the temptation to woolgather at those times when there was nothing better to do . . .

If he was so infuriatingly stubborn and self-opinionated to other people, it was perhaps inevitable that his sub-conscious should be an extention of the character that he projected to strangers . . .

And there was certainly nothing better to do tonight while he was a prisoner in the lock-up of a town that was so serenely peaceful he could hear somebody rhythmically snoring . . .

84

That would be the Reverend Michael Masterson in the law office through the open doorway: the preacher's unasked-for duties as a deputy sheriff in charge of a model prisoner not so onerous that he was able to keep awake over the book he had been reading . . .

The Bible, maybe. Which he must have read often before . . .

Adam Steele had read it often enough, or had it read to him, as a churchgoing child and young man back in Virginia. Never since then? The last time he had seen one . . ?

Was it in the hands of the Reverend Saul M Jarvis, the drunken priest who performed his marriage service to Lucy Girard? Surely not. But did it matter . . ?

'I reckon not,' the Virginian murmured aloud, or maybe only thought he voiced the notion. This as he heard a horse leave town at a gallop. Heading east from the eastern end of the street: the thudding of hooves unobtrusive when he first heard the sound and then quickly diminishing as the rider put distance between himself and the Hope Livery Stable from where he had started.

Steele drifted contentedly into a dreamless sleep. And seemed, as he came close to the surface of waking, to have been in that state of effortless limbo for just a few moments before he heard the sound of hooves on hard-packed ground once more. On a rising scale of volume now as the animal galloped in off the east trail and slowed to a stop at the livery. There was a note of distress in the whinny the horse vented at the end of its run. Steele's half awake consciousness queried its own interpretation of what had been heard, and cast doubt on the images that were conjured up. Was there a horse in the night, and if there was how could he be sure it started out from the livery and returned there? Because his own black stallion was stabled there. And if anybody wanted to steal him and run him ragged, there was nothing he—Adam Steele—could do to prevent such a thing. When he was let out of the lock-up . . .

But that was getting him back into the realm of seeking to predict the nebulous future without knowing the salient facts about present circumstances . . .

He began to allow sleep to blot out that area of his mind that he liked to consider capable of logical thought processes. Knew that his sub-conscious was in control of whatever images would come to him if no other outside influences disturbed him. Realised he was closer to waking than to sleeping as, following the cry of the horse, he heard a clock strike five times. It was the clock in the shack across from the Pioneer at the far western end of the street. Such was the perfect peace of Rosarita, the chimes of the clock sounded over a distance that was close to half a mile.

It could not have been much after ten o'clock last night when he went to sleep and now it was close to dawn. So much for the notion that the dreamless sleep had lasted for just a few moments . . .

Seven hours was usually more than adequate for the Virginian, even after a long day in the saddle enduring whatever the elements and the terrain combined to range against him. But this morning he felt a strong desire to keep his eyes closed against the first light of a new day. And was sure that the balance would soon be weighted on the side of more sleep.

But then a man yelled something. He was down the street close to where the horse had ended the gallop. What he shouted could not be discerned because the words were muffled by distance. He sounded shocked. The horse gave vent to a whole series of whinnies. Doors were wrenched open and more voices were raised. Men and women. Angry, afraid or curious. Dogs barked and babies cried. Footfalls beat on side-walks and porches and the street. Again the hooves of a lone horse could be heard. Then much of the noise faltered and faded and the shouting of one man could

86

be heard clearly against the thudding of the hooves. Both the diminishing volume of the extraneous sounds and the fact that the man and the horse were coming closer enabled Steele to gain an initial impression of what was happening. This as he eased himself tentatively up off the cot and to his feet—grimacing at the pains in his belly and legs but able to keep from groaning.

'. . . the Nelson boy's geldin'! Took him outta the stable late last night! Bad mouthed me for askin' questions! Now look at him! I ain't never seen so much blood! I don't know what this town's acomin' to when this kinda . . .'

Steele was at the window, gripping the bars as he flexed his muscles and tested the joints in those areas of his body that had taken the brunt of Kyle's viciousness. While he ran this check on himself and concluded that he did not need very much healing time, he surveyed the scene on the street that was lit by the murky grey light of the false dawn. Saw a scrawny old man dressed only in dirty longjohns and unlaced boots as he led a sweat-foamed grey gelding by the reins: the horse looking near to exhausted while the dishevelled and unshaven old-timer appeared more vexed than perturbed that his sleep had been interrupted at such an early hour. There were two men and one woman, all three wearing more clothes than the old-timer, hurrying to keep up with him. And perhaps a dozen other Rosarita citizens, mostly men, came into the Virginian's field of vision from the western stretch of the street. The old man allowed his complaint to hang unfinished in the chill air of early morning and everyone shuffled to a halt when the door of the law office was wrenched open and the town preacher demanded to know:

'Now, Matt, what's all this noise about—and just why are you running around on the open street in such a state of undress?'

'Shit, ain't Orville Kyle back yet?' the liveryman growled.

'There's no cause for that language when you're adressin' the Reverend Masterson!' a woman rebuked. 'Especially so when there are ladies present!'

Matt Hope scowled and looked set to snarl a whole stream of obscenities at his fellow citizens, who mostly made sounds of agreement with what had been said. But the preacher hurried to speak ahead of the liveryman. And stepped out of the law office doorway to move toward the winded horse as he announced:

'The sheriff expects to be back this morning. Until then, I am his deputy. Now, precisely what . . . Oh, dear God in heaven what could have happened?'

As the gathering of curious bystanders in various stages of undress grew larger, the cassock-garbed man came close enough to the dejected horse to see that Hope had not been exaggerating.

'It's like I was sayin',' the liveryman replied, and over-emphasised his calm and collected manner now as he swept his sunken-eyed gaze back and forth over the expectantly frowning faces of his quietly enlarging audience. 'This here is Pierce Nelson's mount. The boy came to my place late last night, just when I was about to bed myself down. When I asked him, interested like, where he planned on goin' that time of night he told me to . . . Well, since there's ladies and the minister here, I won't tell you what he says to me.'

'Get on with it, Matt!' somebody urged.

'Duncan Nelson ain't there. He oughta hear this!'

'Go bring him, Leroy,' a man ordered and Steele recognised the voice of James Bate.

'You bet!' his tall, broad and good-looking son offered eagerly. And began to run toward the Pioneer.

'And best bring Doc Bascomb!' Fraser Sorrel from the stage and telegraph office called after the loping youngster. Then explained to a curious neighbour:

'Ought to be able to tell from the amount and kind of blood how bad the boy's been hurt.'

'Can I get finished and be done with this business, do you mind?' Matt Hope asked sourly. He accepted the silence of his audience for an answer and went on: 'Heard a horse out front of my place just now and knew from the sound of him he wasn't in such good shape. Stepped outside and found Pierce Nelson's geldin'. Almost the way you see him now. Sweat wasn't dried and he was breathin' a lot worse. Blood on the saddle and his right flank was just as dried up. About it. Brought him down here to show Orville Kyle. Since he ain't in town, I guess it's right that the boy's Pa should have a look-see and decide what's to be done about his son. Me, I want to tend to the animal's needs soon as I'm allowed.'

Steele had been standing on one leg at a time as he raised and lowered the foot of the other one to exercise his knees. Now he let go of the supporting window bars and turned to walk back and forth along the cell: and was able to show a quiet smile of satisfaction that the degree of his various pains had diminished to nothing more than mild discomforts. While he was discovering this there was an eruption of competing voices on the street as the light of the new day brightened: people asking questions, others offering opinions and still more disagreeing.

Then, against the clapping of hands to gain attention, the preacher employed his pulpit tone of voice to implore: 'Please, please, gentlemen, ladies! I think it best if everyone returns home—to get properly attired if for no other purpose. Meanwhile, I will make preparations to leave——'

'Holy Moses, Michael Masterson!' Ellie Webb cut in. 'Orville Kyle never meant for you to take that deputy nonsense so serious as this!'

'That's right, Mr Masterson!'

'I should think so! Imagine, the Reverend Masterson

89

thinkin' he has to go out the Lord knows where to look for that fool kid!'

'What kinda town is this? We surely have enough men more fitted to——'

'Hey, here comes Dunc Nelson!'

This last was shouted by Earl Webb, who needed to add raucousness to his tone so that his voice commanded attention against the barrage of others. Then, after a few moments of tense silence as everyone peered to the west—along stretched shadows cast by the leading arc of the rising sun—a woman rasped in a hush whisper:

'He looks real sick. I reckon Leroy Bate must've——'

'He looks sick the same way Henry Bascomb looks sick, Lucy,' a man broke in, his tone reproachful. 'Like they both have trouble seein' straight and puttin' one foot in front of the other—and keepin' in their bellies the liquor they put away last night!'

The man who recognised the visible symptoms of a hangover gradually lowered his voice as the saloon-keeper and the doctor drew closer. This as the main body of bystanders opened up a corridor through which the men who were so unsteady on their feet, and the arrogantly strutting Leroy Bate, could pass. Masterson made to offer an explanation of what he had heard had taken place, but the short and fat, late middle-aged Duncan Nelson gestured with an emphatic wave of his hand that the preacher should hold his tongue. Then, as the young Bate was forced to a chagrined halt by his father's hand hooked over a shoulder, the saloonkeeper and Bascomb advanced on the horse. Both the obviously hungover men were dressed in the way Steele had last seen them when they brought him to the law office and thence to the lock-up. But their clothes were creased and wrinkled in a way that provided a match with their faces under unkempt thinning hair. So it seemed a fair assumption that they had fallen into drunken stupors when their liquor-sodden minds demanded rest—not so long ago.

90

'Leroy Bate told us,' Nelson said, enunciating his words with the same degree of slow caution that now guided his steps.

'Hell of a thing,' the town doctor muttered, his voice slurred and his purple-veined nose looking even uglier in the glitteringly bright sunlight of a fresh new morning.

The gelding, almost run into the ground, stood utterly still in pathetic dejection as Matt Hope sidled away to the left and the preacher backed off to the right. And Henry Bascomb moved in close, apparently having some difficulty in focussing his eyes; while the saloon-keeper merely treated the hapless horse to a baleful look before he turned carefully around to face the largest concentration of his fellow citizens. Rocked from side to side and scowled with irritation until he had regained his balance on legs that were splayed some three feet apart. Only then admitted:

'If Pierce is dead, like all that spilled blood seems to show he is, I killed him!'

'All this blood, dead is what the guy who lost it is likely to be,' the town doctor announced.

This caused the tears that had welled into Nelson's eyes to erupt over the lower lids and cascade down his flabby cheeks. Then the saloonkeeper brought his pudgy hands up to his face as another burst of talk from many throats started to fill the sunlit morning air: conflicting tones suggesting that half the people were trying to console Duncan Nelson while the other half were bawling out Doc Bascomb for his lack of tact. Movements accompanied the vocal noise, as the bystanders closed in on the weeping saloonkeeper and the abruptly shamefaced doctor. And the scrawny old man who ran the town livery led the weary horse off down the street in the kind of surreptitious manner that indicated he was expecting to hear a snarled order that he should stop what he was doing. The Reverend Masterson also turned his back on the centre of attention. And looked

91

as if he were intent upon gazing up at the clear morning sky with a plea for divine guidance. But perhaps because he had lived long enough in the material world to have been denied such an easy solution too often before, he agreed willingly to be drawn by a crooked finger to the window of the Virginian's cell.

'Sir?'

'It's morning feller.'

'I'm afraid I fail——'

'You heard the sheriff. He planned to be back this morning and to turn me loose.'

Not every curious watcher had moved to form a tightknit group around Nelson and Bascomb. Ellie Webb was one of thse who did not and she came to stand alongside Masterson out front of the lock-up. Confirmed:

'That's what Orville Kyle said sure enough.'

'But he also said that if something cropped up that I felt I could not take care of then I should——'

'Said help wouldn't be slow in coming, as I recall,' the banker's wife cut in, her tone and manner grimly resolute in contrast with the way the preacher's voice trembled and he tried desperately not to look anybody in the eye. 'So I'm here to help, Michael Masterson and I say you should let Mr Steele out of the lock-up.'

For a stretched second the pale, hollow-cheeked face of the preacher looked to be hardening into an expression of determination to assert his authority. But then, abruptly, there was an ominous silence as the voice of Duncan Nelson commanded:

'Hold it.'

High tension had an almost palpable presence in the warming, brightening air of the morning as the preacher and the woman turned to look with the Virginian toward the press of people. Nobody in the crowd looked back at the face between the bars and the man and woman flanking the lock-up window.

'Leroy is right!' the saloonkeeper went on and didn't

seem to have to work at keeping the confusing effects of too much liquor out of his voice now. 'If Orville ain't here to take care of this business, we got to do it ourselves. Any man wants to join us, be at the livery and ready to ride at six!'

There was a roar of approval and a less vociferous burst of talk against the call to action as the gathering suddenly broke up. And some Rosarita citizens hurried with a will to be ready in good time for the appointed hour while others moved off with dragging feet and shaking heads. Few cast more than an indifferent glance in the direction of the lock-up. And it was with an air of being rebuffed that the preacher brought his head around to announce:

'Very well, I think you are correct, Mrs Webb. I had charge solely of Mr Steele. The sheriff did, I know, say he was to be released this morning. Once that is done, my duties as a deputy have been discharged.'

Masterson strode purposefully toward the law office doorway and Ellie Webb trailed him, pointedly ignoring an enquiring gaze that her husband directed at her. The rotund little banker with the weak-looking face was by then the only figure who remained on the centre of the street between the law office and the unfinished hotel as the crowd that once had been there dispersed. For several moments he gazed at the doorway through which his wife had gone, his expression apprehensive: like he doubted the wisdom of her prominent involvement in the town's trouble. Then he sensed the Virginian eyeing him impassively and at once was guiltily embarrassed—as if he felt Steele had been able to read what was in his mind. He said hurriedly:

'You shouldn't judge Rosarita folks on what you've seen of them during this time of trouble, Mr Steele.'

'I shouldn't?' Steele countered as he heard footfalls behind him and glanced over his shoulder to see the banker's wife pushing a key into the lock of the cell door.

'Well, you've seen only one side of them,' Earl Webb insisted as Steele picked his hat off the cot and donned it.

'Yeah, feller,' the Virginian agreed evenly as he glanced out through the bars again. 'Backsides I reckon.'

'Yes, the black side is one way of putting——'

'He said backsides, Earl!' Ellie Webb growled disdainfully through the window at her husband as Steele turned away from it to go out of the cell.

'Grateful to you people for helping me out, the Virginian said as he paused on the threshold between the lock-up and the law office and showed a less than warm smile to both the woman and the preacher. 'It's lucky for me everyone in town isn't an asshole.'

9

Adam Steele rode out of Rosarita and onto the east
trail as the first of the vigilantes began to gather out
front of Matt Hope's livery stable. Leroy Bate was in
the group, eager to make tracks. His taller but much
less powerfully built father was also on the street with a
saddled horse, but looked like he would much rather be
back preparing to open up his grocery store. Frank
Sorrel did a lot of nervous tugging at his bushy moustache
while he waited. Just three other men the Virginian
recognised from yesterday's saloon deputation and this
morning's gathering outside the law office were also in
a position to say something to him when he led the
black stallion out of the livery, swung up into the saddle
and heeled his mount forward. But nobody spoke and
only the Bate boy gave the Virginian anything more
than a passing glance that ranged from apologetic to
something close to envious. The youngster glared with
his eyes and sneered with his mouth and continued to
watch the departing rider for long seconds while the
older men peered in the opposite direction: perhaps
hoping that the saloonkeeper had changed his mind and
would come to the livery only to announce that he had
decided to wait for the return of the sheriff.

Out beyond the sign that was the eastern town limits
marker—it welcomed strangers to Rosarita with neat
and quite recently freshly painted lettering—Steele
sensed that there were suddenly more than one pair of
eyes fixed upon him, and he turned in the saddle while
he continued to have his mount walk easily along the
heavily used trail. It was a long way back now to the

livery, beyond the cemetery, the stage and telegraph office and the Webbs' bank and so it was not possible to discern the expressions on the faces of the men grouped there. Nor was the Virginian able to recognise any of the men, walking or slowly riding horses, who were heading along the street toward the livery. He could guess that Duncan Nelson was on the street, equipped for what might turn out to be a dangerous ride: but if Leroy Bate was still glaring at him with unconcealed hostility, Steele could no longer sense it. The men with the youngster were all peering at a point on the trail beyond the lone rider—where it swung to the south and curved out of sight behind a stand of pines. And as he turned his impasssive attention to the same direction he knew that most of the men were seeking—with faint hope of seeing it—a first glimpse of Orville Kyle as the lawman returned toward town.

The Virginian did not look behind him again until he had ridden around the curve of the trail: and then he only did so as a part of his habitual survey of the terrain, his dark eyes searching for anything that might signal danger. He saw nothing that caused him to do a fast double-take as he tensed himself to abandon the reins for the stock and frame of the Colt Hartford jutting from the forward hung boot. And neither did his not always trustworthy sense for lurking menace give him reason to itch between the shoulderblades or sweat more heavily than the rising heat of the morning required.

He did not sweat very much at all after he had taken off his suit jacket and stowed it under the same tie that lashed his sheepskin coat to his bedroll. For the trail over most of its constantly curving and rising and falling route was shaded by the towering pines that flanked it. And he elected to ride at an easy walk that did not exert himself or his mount. There was no reason for this pace other than that it suited his purpose and his mood. This purpose was to get the feel of the timber-rich country through which he was moving: in much the same way as he tested how he felt about Rosarita even after his first run-in with the sheriff. His mood as he rode easily along the shaded trail, breathing cool air fragrant with the scent of the pines, was of quiet satisfaction with his present circumstances.

He was out of the lock-up, the discomforts of the beating were diminishing by the minute and the uncustomary trouble that was causing so much unrest in Rosarita had only involved him because of the way he had *infuriated* Orville Kyle with his *self-opinionated stubbornness*. Steele felt so contented with his lot this morning he was prepared to admit this to himself, and even crack one of his one-time boyish grins as he did so. Contributing to his pleasantly complacent frame of mind was the fact that he and his horse were well fed and completely rested due to Kyle's own intransigence and Matt Hope's conscientious competence as a liveryman. And for no charge—for neither Ellie Webb nor Hope had asked for payment and Steele had certainly not offered to cover the cost of his supper and for the stabling, feed and curry combing the stallion had received. He had been aware ever since he was put in the lock-up that the travelling money he carried in his pockets had not been touched. And his first act when the preacher returned his gear to him in the law office was to check the contents of his saddlebags to ensure the sack of gold nuggets worth around five thousand dollars, and another eight thousand in bills remained intact.

'Whatever was in there when your possessions were brought here will be in there now,' Masterson had said solemnly as he watched Steele go through the bags, a look of injured dignity in his sunken eyes. 'Whatever else he may be, the sheriff is not a thief.'

'Same as the whole town, young man,' Ellie Webb had added, her homely features set in a frown of earnestness. 'Whoever brought your stuff in the office wouldn't have touched it for any other reason than to tote it.'

But the Virginian had double checked anyway: and ensured that the preacher and the woman did not see the gold nuggets and the bundle of cash money that was his current stake to get him started in the horse ranching business. He had done the counting in such a manner that it could not be seen by the reproachful eyes of the sincere couple because it was in his nature to trust nobody. Was so ingrained that he would remain suspicious of his fellow man for the rest of his life—even if he were to find the perfect piece of land to ranch and thereafter come into contact only with people as ardently honest as was claimed for the citizens of Rosarita. For although such an eagerly desired change in the style of his life would surely result in some shifts of his personality, certain facets of his character he knew would never alter.

But this was not a newly discovered strain of self-awareness, and so the line of thought did not mar his peace of mind as he rode out of the band of timber some two miles as the crow flies from town. Reined his horse to a halt and swept his gaze over a broad vista of grass-covered rolling hills featured by nature with out-croppings of rock and stands of timber, and by man with farmsteads. Close to where Steele sat his horse, on the rim of the first of many shallow and broad valleys that corrugated the terrain for as far as he could see, there were four places that were still being worked. There were two on one side of the trail and two on the other side. Each place was fenced and had a house and a barn and corral with fields of healthy looking crops on all sides. There was at least one horse in each corral, along with a milk cow. On one place there were some hogs in a pen and on another there were chickens. Each had a well in the front yard and all had a column of smoke rising straight from the house chimney. At least one man worked in the fields of each farmstead and

98

without exception they raised a hand in greeting as Steele rode down into the valley and among the places without pausing. He responded in a like manner to these men, and to an old-timer who waved as he sat in a rocker on a porch. Once he tipped his hat toward a woman who came out of her house to go to the well just as he was passing. The houses, which all showed signs of having been extended from crude beginnings over the years, and the men working the fields, were too far back from the trail to make it easy for an exchange of the time of day. But Steele was conscious of the tacit friendliness of the farming families and detected no sense of being watched with surreptitious curiosity when his back was toward those people he had or had not seen. So either news of the stranger to town had not reached out into this part of the country yet, or these farming people were uninterested in the troubles of Rosarita.

On the far side of this first valley he rode under an arch of sun-bleached rough timber with a plank fixed to the cross-member. On the plank was a just discernible painted legend: PUBLIC ROAD ACROSS PRIVATE LAND—OWNED BY A BEGLEY. Beyond the arch the trail looped up and over the rise into another valley where there had once been a half dozen farmsteads that were larger, and therefore more widely scattered, than those which were still being worked. But, as Steele had been told in town, these had been bought up by Avery Begley many years earlier: and since then they had fallen into a state of dereliction in the same way as the place beside the cottonwoods on the river bank out on the far side of Rosarita. Just a crumbling wall here and a chimney there, a leaning line of fencing, a wagon with only one wheel and a child's swing suspended on rusted iron chains from a tree branch gave clues to how men and women had once worked this piece of terrain and been successful enough at their labours to establish homes and begin to raise families. For the rest, nature had resumed control and grass and brush and young saplings had taken hold on the once cultivated fields.

In the third valley there was still visible the sign of just one abandoned farmstead. But perhaps there had been more and maybe relics of them were still to be found, if anyone were interested, among the many stands of timber that were the dominant natural feature of this piece of country. And it was in this valley, where the trail turned sharply to the right and began to drop gently down into a brush and timber crowded ravine that Steele found Pierce Nelson.

The sixteen-year-old boy lay face down in the brush at the side of the trail, legs together and arms at his sides. The Virginian recognised him because of the Stetson that was still held between his shoulderblades by the thong around his neck. The kid had put on a duster for his night ride into the country. There was no blood staining the back of the cream-coloured coat. Because the night had been chill, and so far this morning the spot where the body lay had remained in the shade of the trees, decomposition had been arrested. So Pierce Nelson had not started to stink yet. But that the boy was dead Steele had no doubt from the moment he saw the total inertia of the form. And the stallion was just a moment later in sensing death was in the air: snorted and tossed his head nervously as his rider reined him in. But the horse calmed to the gentle touch of a gloved hand on his neck and then the softly spoken words as the Virginian swung out of the saddle. The animal needed no urging to be led to the far side of the trail where Steele hitched the reins to a clump of four-foot high sagebrush.

The Virginian felt confident enough that he was alone with the dead boy to leave his rifle in the boot as he moved back toward the body, taking the time to note the most obvious sign on the trail. Then he stooped over the corpse and used both hands and the steadying lever of a lower leg and foot to ease Pierce

100

Nelson from belly down to face up: with much the same delicacy as he would have applied had the boy been alive and badly hurt.

He looked a lot older than sixteen, and the aging process of dying the hard way had caused his acne scarred face to become ugly. He had been skinny when he was alive and now that he was dead he seemed almost emaciated. His thin lips were tightly compressed and his eyes were open to their fullest extent: and they looked greener than when life had animated them. The expression in the eyes, frozen there at the instant of dying, showed the agony of suffering rather than anguish that the end had come so soon in his life.

The cause of his death was a bullet in his belly. It had gone through his duster just above the lowest button that had been fastened and had made a neat little hole in the fabric. The stain of a massive blood loss was not so neat in the way it had blossomed irregularly out around three sides of the hole: to the fourth side the blood had spurted and then seeped down over his saddle and horse.

As Steele straightened up from the corpse without peering more closely at the wound, his bristled face was expressionless. And when he turned and then hunkered down to examine from close quarters the sign on the trail, his eyes narrowed just a fraction in concentration and he drew back his lips to expose teeth through which he allowed a tuneless whistle to escape softly. A few moments later he came upright and moved along the trail for twenty or so paces, bent forward from the waist, and with his neck craned so that he was better able to see the tiny areas of shadow that the early morning sun cast among the sign. Then he returned to the point on the trail between the corpse of Pierce Nelson and his uneasy horse, double-checked his initial conclusion and was fairly sure he had read the scarce sign correctly.

The youngster had been shot someplace to the east

of where he died. Then, by choice or because his horse was spooked by the gunfire, he headed back for town at a gallop. He made it as far as the end of the ravine before he was unseated and was thrown to the trail. He had dragged himself off the trail and into the brush. How long the boy had remained there before he died Steele could not guess. But the degree of agony expressed in his eyes could not have been torturing him for very long—for he had not thrashed around or spilled much blood after he crawled to the spot where he died. Perhaps he had lost consciousness for a time? But conjecture was pointless, Steele told himself as he unfastened the ties of his bedroll. Apart from the fact that Pierce Nelson had died here as a result of a stomach wound, the only other certainty about what had happened in the night was that the kid had had company for awhile.

This was a man who also rode here from the east, dismounted and sat in the brush at the boy's side. Chewed some tobacco and did some spitting of juice-coloured saliva. And did a little bleeding of his own. Before, the sign seemed to indicate, he spooked the dead youngster's horse into a bolt for Rosarita then climbed back into the saddle of his own mount to ride off to the east, dripping spots of blood into the dust of the trail.

While the Virginian unfurled his bedroll and used a blanket to drape the corpse, he found it impossible to bar from his mind the facts that Sheriff Orville Kyle had left Rosarita ahead of Pierce Nelson yesterday and that the lawman was a tobacco chewer. But, as he refixed his depleted bedroll behind his saddle and then unhitched the stallion from the sagebrush, he found it easy to resist the temptation to speculate on the basis of what could be a false premise formed by coincidence.

And it was none of his business, either. Let the dead boy's father and the bunch of vigilantes he was leading out from town get to the bottom of the mysterious

102

killing. If the most fervent members of the posse were able to sustain their initial enthusiasm and keep riding this far out of town, Steele had not made any kind of haste, and yet as he swung into the saddle and pressed on along the trail through the ravines there was still no sign of Duncan Nelson and the rest of the men closing on him. But, beyond the ravine and riding up another gentle incline out of a shallow valley, he was again able to easily suppress an initial impulse to wonder what was keeping the posse. And soon he was feeling as contentedly satisfied with life as he had before he found the corpse of the boy.

The open range across which he rode, where the only signs of man's encroachment was now the trail and its accompanying telegraph wire, looked to be just the kind of country for which he was seeking. Well watered bunch grass grazing land upon which stock of a man's choosing could not do anything else but thrive. Unspectacular country scenically, but pretty enough to look at for a man as materialistically minded as Adam Steele. The nearest neighbours as far away as a man elected them to be by the siting of his house. Likewise the town where he would have to go for essential supplies every now and then.

Yes, the Begley place certainly seemed to be well suited for his purpose. But, the present trouble apart, it probably was not ideal in all respects. After all, perfection was reputed not to exist this side of the gates to heaven—and he had no desire to feel that brand of utter contentment while he was alive anyway. So if it turned out that Avery Begley's heirs were unwilling to sell off a part of this fine piece of rangeland to him, the Virginian would not be overly concerned by their decision. For there was a big country spread out beyond the crest of every hill, and what was yet to be seen over the next rise could well be even better than what seemed to be so good right now. So if Charlotte and Dale Begley turned down the offer he intended to make them . . . well, at least he had seen that the kind of place he was looking for did exist outside of his imagination.

Despite having adamantly acknowledged to himself that local troubles were none of his concern, Steele could not fail to register that he was still following the sign left by the man who had sat beside the dead or dying Pierce Nelson for a period last night. He saw, too, where the eastward ride of the boy had been halted by the gunshot that blasted a hole in his belly and his horse wheeled and commenced the gallop back the way he had come. Here, also, beside a dark outcrop of red rock, the tobacco chewer had started to bleed. Steele noticed such signs as he maintained his customary survey of his surroundings: and as before he found it easy not to speculate. But then, some thirty minutes of easy riding away from the corpse, he reached a spur trail and could no longer ignore what the sign on the hard-packed dirt told him.

The spur cut off the trail to the north, curving out of sight into an extensive stand of mixed timber. A board was nailed to a tree trunk at a side of the spur. It hung askew on rusted nails and the crudely painted lettering was just discernible after many years of weather had done their worst to wash and bleach away the warning: *KEEP OUT—By Order. Avery Begley.* There was no easy-to-spot sign that the cut-under buggy and the flatbed wagon rented from Matt Hope in Rosarita had turned in off the main trail. But Steele could not fail to see that the tobacco chewer had swung off onto the spur here. He had not dripped any spots of blood for a considerable way, but he had continued to spit juice-coloured saliva at irregular intervals.

So, as he tugged gently on the reins to steer the stallion out of the full glare of the mid-morning sun and into the dappled shade of the timber, Steele was forced by the dictates of commonsense to acknowledge it was unlikely he could remain apart from the past and

104

present troubles that were none of his concern. They had started here on the Begley property and the tobacco-chewing man who knew something about the way Pierce Nelson died had apparently brought them back. Somewhere back on the trail—and surely the posse could not be too far distant by now?—the saloon-keeper and his fellow citizens could not fail to see the sign that marked an easy-to-follow trail between the corpse and the spur along which the Virginian now rode.

Hell, he was a fool to even contemplate the prospect of talking buying and selling business in such cir-cumstances. But, like it had been said of him, he was infuriatingly stubborn and self-opinionated. And, also like it had been said, nothing that is worthwhile comes easy. He spat at a tobacco juice stain at the side of the trail. He missed it, but this would only have mattered if he had believed in omens and such like. So he simply scowled, without being entirely sure why: then his face became impassive as he rode out of the timber and toward two stout posts between which a gate had once hung. Now, and for a long time beforehand, the rotting remains of the gate lay off to the side, at the corner of a weed-choked field—one of several that stretched back from the gateless entrance in a line of mostly fallen down fencing toward a huddle of buildings in the bottom of a hollow some quarter of a mile away.

Because the farmstead where Avery Begley had chosen to live was in a hollow, the Virginian was able to gain an excellent first impression of the place from his elevated vantage point after he had reined in his stallion at the gateway. There was a stone-walled, timber-roofed house that looked only big enough to contain two rooms. It was in need of maintenance, but was not in such a bad state of disrepair as the larger barn with a hayloft in the steeply pitched roof. Out back of the house, in the area between it and the barn there were some small animal houses with fenced enclosures.

The fields to either side of the house and outbuildings—ditches, hedges and lines of timber showed how the ground had once been sub-divided—were as overgrown as those that flanked the wagon-wide strip of hard-packed ground between the gateway and the front yard of the place. Out back was the land that Avery Begley had cultivated. This was fenced on all four sides, and except where the fencing had been flattened at two places—both some three hundred feet wide— the enclosure looked to be well maintained: the posts treated with creosote not so long ago and the strands of wire gleaming in the sunlight so obviously not rusted. Between the two gaps in the fence, from the north back to the west side a great swathe of destruction had been laid by a large herd of stampeding cattle. Maize, wheat, root vegetables and beans had suffered under the trampling hooves of the animals as they thundered across the land of one man that was coveted by another.

Nowhere on Begley land had Steele seen signs of the grass fires that Hart might have ordered lit. But beyond the north west corner of the fenced area he saw sunlight glinting on a body of water. There was a fence encircling this and he thought this could be the fishing pool that Ellie Webb said was poisoned by Lucas Hart's men.

To the north and east of the farmstead the terrain rose in a shallow incline cloaked by lush looking grass. Then, close to the crest of the rise, small outcrops of rock jutted drunkenly out of the rich soil. There was just one area, about fifty feet across, where there were no rocky obstacles featuring the top of the slope. And it was here that the cows had started their downward rush toward the Begley place, their pumping hooves churning up the grassland without the animals being in any danger of crashing into and over the dangerous rocks—which the frontrunners would not have been able to see until they came over the ridge at full tilt.

106

Again, the Virginian could not fail to take note of the obvious as he heeled his mount away from the gateposts and down into the hollow on the long time unworked side of the farmstead. But he made no attempt to extend what he saw into a theory about the stampede that led to the death of the man who was the newest occupant in the Rosarita cemetery—would remain so for just a short while before Pierce Nelson assumed the unenviable distinction.

He saw there was smoke curling lazily from the chimney that rose up the outside of one end of the house. He also saw that the buggy and the wagon had been negligently parked on the front yard, apparently left where they came to rest. The horses were apparently in the ramshackle barn. The flatbed had been unloaded of luggage. All that moved down in the bottom of the hollow was the smoke from the chimney and there were no sounds loud enough to be heard above the regular clop of the stallion's hooves against the hard-packed dirt.

If the final quarter mile of trail from town to the front yard of the Begley place showed sign that the tobacco chewer had ridden over the same route a few hours earlier, Steele had no inclination to look for it. Because his sense for impending trouble was sounding an indistinct warning somewhere in a dark recess of his consciousness. Indistinct because the farmstead was a troubled place anyway, by all accounts, and the sign he had followed since he discovered the corpse of the kid emphasised that trouble had not ended when the fatally sick Avery Begley was carried away from here.

It looked fine. Not ideal: but like the country he had ridden through to get here, this place could be made to suit his purpose. It would need a lot of work to fix it up, but it certainly had the potential.

He was within a hundred and fifty feet of the firmly closed front door of the crude house. Still attempting to quell what he considered to be unfounded uneasiness by looking at the place from the point of view of possibly owning it. But he was so tensed to respond to sudden danger that he started to hurt in places that had not suffered in the beating he took yesterday. And then a scowl displaced impassivity on his unshaven face. This as he reined the stallion to an abrupt halt. Had no time to thrust his right hand forward to fist it around the stock of the Colt Hartford as the door of the house was wrenched open. And the elder of Charlotte Begley's escorts stood on the threshold: a Winchester rifle aimed from the shoulder.

'You surprise me, sir,' he greeted in an even tone.

'You gave me something of a start,' Steele countered.

'I may smile at your humour when the situation is less fraught with anxiety on all sides, Mr . . ?'

'Adam Steele, feller.'

'Fletcher Arness, Mr Steele. Your presence here surprises me because you struck me as a man of some intelligence when we first met in town yesterday. I assumed you were not the kind of man who needed to be told anything more than once?'

With the cocked rifle held in a rock-steady aim at the Virginian's chest, Arness's attitude remained as effortlessly well-mannered as it had been at the Webbs' bank. And the expression on his leanly handsome, evenly bronzed, clean shaven, blue-eyed face was the same as it had been then—just a hairsbreadth removed from lighting with a friendly smile. But, Steele was certain, he was the kind of man who was able to kill with such a look of amiability toward his victim. Today he was not wearing a derby, cravat or suit jacket. But he nonetheless exuded elegance with boots that were highly sheened, pants that were perfectly pressed, a vest with polished buttons and a shirt that was stiffly starched. The metallic buttons of the vest and the matching fasteners at his shirt cuffs provided the only note of contrast with the otherwise solid blackness of his garb.

'No offence, but the lady doesn't interest me, except as the owner of this place now that Avery Begley's dead.'

'Miss Begley might be offended to hear you say that. I accept what you say in the manner you have said it. In return, I would ask you to take no for an answer this second time of asking. Miss Charlotte Begley has no intention of selling this property she inherited from the previous owner. So I think it best you be on your way to look for what you want elsewhere, Mr Steele. With my apologies for the lack of hospitality. Unfortunately, we are not yet in a position to entertain guests. Having just moved here from the city, as you know.'

Steele nodded, then said: 'One thing, feller?'

'If it will not take long.'

'You always see off unwanted visitors with a rifle?'

'Just those who I feel will not be persuaded by a simple word of caution, Mr Steele.' Now the near smile suddenly became closer to the scowl he had worn as he drove the buggy out of Rosarita yesterday. And an icy tone entered his voice when he added: 'I spoke to you in town, and so . . .' He raised the shoulder that did not support the rifle stock.

Steele felt irritably dissatisfied that he had to let this be the end of it. It was the Begley woman he had come to see, but it was obvious he would have to start trouble with Fletcher Arness to get to her. Was it worth the risk? She had sounded adamant in Rosarita before she saw the place she had inherited. Before he had seen it, either. Was she still as determined as the dandy with the rifle maintained now she had seen what there was to hold on or to sell? Also, how strong was his hankering to settle on this piece of country so well suited to raising horses—now that he was looking down the barrel of yet another gun on account of his interest? What aggravated him so much was that he found both questions equally impossible to resolve right then. And, because he could feel his anger expanding and knew there was a danger of it altering from cold to hot, he decided to back off and gain time to think.

'A thought to ride with you, Mr Steele,' Fletcher Arness said, his tone even and his expression almost a smile again as he watched the faintly frowning Virginian start to wheel the black stallion.

'I've got plenty of my own, feller,' the Virginian answered.

'You can carry one more. Just want you to keep in mind that I've never shot a man in the back. So provided you keep heading away from me, you have nothing to worry about: as far as I'm concerned.'

Steele needed to take a moment to bring under control the impulse to a flare of anger that in the present circumstances would be either reckless or futile. And managed to achieve this behind a mask of impassivity as he further sought to conceal the depth of his feelings toward Arness by raising a gloved hand and flicking a forefinger against the underside of the brim. Then thought his voice sounded just a little strained when he tried for an even tone as he replied:

'I hope the lady's as impressed as I am, feller.'

Charlotte Begley let a trill of laughter escape her smiling mouth as she moved into the doorway at Arness's side and then called: 'Fletcher never fails to amaze me, Mr Steele! Perhaps when he does there may be a place for you here!'

It was not far away from noon and the woman was still in a nightgown of some fine white fabric that was diaphanous, but decently draped her body because it was so full from neck to ankles. Her red hair hung freely to below her shoulders and was tousled from sleep but she had done something to take most of the signs of the night off her face. This morning she no longer looked regal: instead merely an attractive woman of early middle age indulging an inclination for a brand of coquettishness that did not become her.

'Miss Begley sometimes makes jokes at the wrong

time, too,' Arness said sardonically as Steele extended the flick of his hat brim to become a more genteel tipping of his Stetson now that the woman had shown herself.

Then Dale Begley snarled from inside the dilapidated house: 'Goddamnit, Fletch! The bastard's got a friggin' army with him!'

A gunshot and the shattering of a window as the bullet exploded through the glass momentarily transfixed the attention of Steele astride his wheeling horse and the couple in the doorway. In that part of a second, Arness and the woman snapped their heads to the side to look at the fear-filled youngster who had fired the shot. And the Virginian gazed at the shower of glass shards sprayed out of the frame to splash across the yard.

'You jerk, I gave him my word——' Fletcher Arness started to snarl as he snapped his head around again. And was in time to see Steeele thud his heels against the flanks of the stallion to lunge the animal into an instant gallop.

'No, he's right!' the woman shrieked, thrusting an arm with a pointing finger out through the doorway. 'Look at them! Get him, Dale! That's my boy!'

The Virginian, the hair at the nape of his neck still standing up after the bullet brushed through it, rasped through clenched teeth as a barrage of gunfire masked all other sounds: 'That sure makes him a sonofabitch!'

10

More glass shattered under the impact of perhaps more than one bullet. And the door of the house was slammed closed as the fusillade of shots thudded into wood or ricocheted off the stone wall. Steele saw this because he just happened to be looking toward the house when he demanded and got the controlled bolt from his mount. He was crouched in the saddle—leaning far forward in an instinctive attitude that simply meant he was a horizontal rather than a vertical target, but nonetheless made him feel a little safer.

As he saw the door crashed shut and the other window in the front of the house shattered—the shards showering inside the room this time—he got his bearings on where the barrage of gunfire was coming from. And he snatched a glance back up the hill. Had to crane his head around to the limit since the stallion was bolting flat out in the direction he faced when the order to wheel was countermanded. Which meant he was racing across the overgrown fields, heading wide of the south west corner of the house. And although he felt a painful snap in his neck because he had elected to look over the wrong shoulder in the heat of the dangerous moment, he saw enough to know why the Begley boy had taken the shot at him after the claim that an army was about to launch an attack on the house.

It was the posse of vigilantes from Rosarita who were galloping their mounts down into the hollow, rifles and revolvers directing a continuous fusillade of shots at the front of the house. Steele saw only part of the line of advance, and this through a veil of gunsmoke. But in the second before he forced his head painfully around to face the way he was going he recognised a half dozen men he could not name, in addition to Fraser Sorrel, Doc Bascomb and Matt Hope.

None of the Rosarita men was firing at him, as far as the Virginian was able to tell. And the incessant gunfire that poured toward the house served to force those inside to stay back from the smashed windows. But Steele did not trust this situation to last from one moment to the next. And he decided to make for cover by the fastest means before a stray shot, a ricochet or a deliberately placed bullet tore into his body.

He sat suddenly upright in the saddle and stepped down hard against the stirrups as he hauled back on the reins with both hands. The stallion snorted in rage at the brutal abruptness of the demand. But, well schooled by his rider over a long period, the animal responded to the best of his ability and began to slither to a halt through the lush green weeds that grew so thickly in the unworked soil. Then the rider jerked sharply on the left rein to command a turn. At the same time as his right hand left the other side of the rein to clasp into a tight fist around the frame of the booted rifle. The horse did his best to make the asked-for turn, but the angle was always too sharp for the speed. And the surface beneath the pumping hooves was slippery with the sap of trampled weeds.

Steele abandoned the final control he had on his mount—released the rein and kicked his feet clear of the stirrups. Then, as the sideways tumble of the stallion became inevitable, he thrust against the horn with his free hand and so was powered out of the saddle. Was thus pitched into a sideways half-somersault across the thick growth of weeds, cushioning to some extent the impact as he crashed to the ground at the same moment as his horse—safely out of danger from the animal's crushing weight.

Just for a second he lay where he had fallen, tensed

113

to experience the agony that would warn of an incapaci-tating injury. But just a few of the former pains from the beating were given new fire. And this level of discomfort left him ample awareness to realise that he was still exposed to the field of fire from the guns of the men galloping their horses down into the hollow. And maybe from a side window of the house in which there were doubtless now three people who were convinced he had set them up for the surprise attack.

He raised his head to get his bearings and vented a grunt of satisfaction when a joint in his neck clicked and at least one area of pain was relieved. Then he briefly smiled when he saw his horse getting up on all fours again, apparently not seriously damaged by the cruel fall he had been forced to take. A glance in the oppo-site direction as the horse trotted away drew another grunt from Steele as he saw that the chimney end wall of the house had no windows in it.

The barrage of gunfire, already considerably dimin-ished, slackened still more as he rolled on to his belly and moved snakelike toward the rear corner of the house. Now the thudding of hooves on the hard-packed dirt and the more muted sounds of horses in the flank-ing fields was more obtrusive than the cracking of gun-shots. The speed of the advance slowed and there was a period of seconds when all the guns were silent.

Steele made it into the cover of the rear wall of the house and rose up on to his haunches, pressing his back against the wall as he took a series of deep breaths and peered across the empty animal enclosures toward the barn that looked as if it might collapse in the first strong wind of winter. He heard men out front of the place yelling at their horses to pull up. Two shots exploded and only now did Steele thumb back the hammer of his rifle.

'Hold it, Dunc!' a Rosarita man bellowed in an angrily commanding tone. 'That's a flag of truce that's bein' shown!'

'I ain't about to talk terms of surrender with the dirty, lowdown, murderin' skunks that killed my boy!' the saloonkeeper retorted and, in the surrounding stillness that seemed to become more palpably heavy with each word spoken by Duncan Nelson, his voice sounded like it was drawing nearer to cracking.

There was a stretched second of total silence in the wake of the threat. Before Dale Begley defended:

'What the frig's he talkin'——'

'Dale, let Fletcher——' the boy's mother broke in and was herself interrupted by Arness.

'There's nobody in here who has killed anybody since we came to these parts! And I intend to defy any man who insists I am a liar by stepping out of the house! Unarmed, I should add! If the man who considers me a liar and one of us a murderer chooses to kill me, then I hope for his sake that he has no conscience to torment him for the rest of his life.'

Steele eased to his full height with the aid of the rifle as a makeshift crutch while he kept his back to the wall—the rough surface of the stonework digging into him through the fabric of his vest and shirt. He discovered he felt no worse discomfort standing than in any other attitude. As he came to his feet, he recognised the voice of the stage and telegraph office manager responding to the arrogant eloquence of Fletcher Arness.

'Hold on, mister! When that door opens, we want to see all of you out here. And all with your hands high so we can see you all have no weapons.'

'Really, sir! Do you honestly feel that a man, a woman and a boy would attempt to get the better of such a large number of——'

'I'm no boy, Fletch!' Dale Begley cut in to protest.

'I'm hardly correctly dressed to meet so many gentlemen and——'

'Quit with the fancy talk mister!' Nelson snarled. 'And I don't care if you're bare-assed naked, woman! We ain't about to trust anythin' about a bunch of city slickers that would gut shoot a kid and toss him into the brush to die!'

There was some more yelling back and forth between the trio trapped in the house and the vigilantes who continued to sit astride their horses in the front yard. And harsh words were also exchanged among the people in the house and on the yard as each group failed to agree on a spokesman and their tactics. But Adam Steele had found his attention diverted elsewhere: and the furore of excited voices was diminished in his mind as he moved away from the rear wall of the dilapidated house and went between the hog pen and chicken run toward the tumbledown barn. But when he reached the centre gap of the part-opened double doors he took the time to glance over his shoulder at the rear wall of the house, in which there was a firmly closed door and no windows. And he knew now that neither the intervening building nor a trick of his mind was muting the raucousness of the quarrelsome voices. The heat had been taken out of the situation at the front of the house. An exchange was still in progress but just two men were talking to each other.

At the front of the barn, the Virginian took a tighter grip with one hand around the frame and the other round the barrel of the Colt Hartford. And felt beads of sweat standing out on his forehead and along his bristled upper lip. When he had first sensed the presence of somebody watching him from within the barn there had been no warning of hostility. But, now that an impression of the threat of violence receding elsewhere had become a reality, he felt less sure of his own safety. He had not been able to pinpoint the spot from where he was being watched in the facade of the barn, and the closer he got to it the more cracks and knot holes he saw through which a malicious eye could be watching him. He saw, too, many areas of rotted timber that would hardly reduce the velocity of a bullet fired through it.

Now that he stood on the threshold of the barn and the main body of noise from beyond the house had subsided, he was aware of the sounds of horses moving in their stalls. He could hear, too, the humming of flies and insects that foraged among the debris within the vacant hog pen and chicken run. And his own measured breathing—that he sought to maintain at the same cadence as he pushed the rifle between the doors before he stepped into the barn.

'You sure are one persistent bastard, aren't you?' Orville Kyle rasped.

The barn was bright with the sunlight that streamed in through the part-opened doors, two almost glassless windows and holes of varying sizes that the elements and neglect had worn into the roof, the floor of the hayloft and all four walls. Thus were the Virginian and the Rosarita sheriff able to see each other with harshly unflattering clarity.

Steele standing in a half-turned, half-crouched attitude at the doorway: his rifle aimed from the hip toward the source of the taunt as his face froze with an expression midway between a grimace of fear and a scowl of anger.

Kyle curled up into a fetal position in the front left corner of the barn, Remington in his holster and his arms akimbo. His head propped up by the angle of the corner and face now turned away from the knot hole through which he had been watching Steele. His features looked to be drained of blood in back of their element burnish, and suffering had cut deep lines into his skin. He seemed to be trying to express smirking contempt for the Virginian, but his duller-than-ever blue-green eyes revealed the awesome level of pain he was experiencing.

'I'm just being myself, feller,' Steele answered, straightening and untensing himself as he canted the Colt Hartford to his shoulder and eased forward the hammer.

117

'I haven't been myself since that crazy Nelson kid put a bullet in my chest,' the lawman said, and pain acted to mask all trace of his Deep South accent as he cautiously unfolded his arms and used his unbandaged hand to pull open his sheepskin coat. Displayed the large stain of dried blood on his shirt front in the area of his silver star.

Steele moved toward the badly injured man as the enstalled horses—just those that had hauled the buggy and flatbed from town yesterday—accepted his presence in the barn and stood in unmoving stillness, but with ears pricked as if they were eager to hear what the intruder had to say.

'Way I read the sign, you stayed around long enough to know the boy isn't feeling anything anymore?'

Now that the Virginian was standing directly over him, Kyle found it difficult to crane his neck into the angle of the walls to look up at him. And he chose to peer out through a knot hole—perhaps seeing the scene beyond or maybe surveying a series of images from his memory—as he confirmed:

'That's what I did, mister. Least I could do, but I'm not sure it made it any easier for the kid. Sure hasn't——'

He grimaced in response to a present physical pain rather than at an ugly memory, and it was forceful enough to curtail his earnestly-spoken response to the Virginian. But then the expression became suddenly less self-centred as a burst of angry talk sounded from out front of the house.

'I only came out here to see about maybe buying——'

'Yeah, I got the drift of that,' the lawman rasped through gritted teeth as somebody—it sounded like Fraser Sorrel—shouted down the townspeople who had become even angrier than before. 'And if I get the drift of what's happening out there, those men from town could finish up as a lynch mob. Stringing up innocent people.'

118

Now he forced his head around and up to direct a questioning look at Steele, who nodded and augmented:

'Reckon so, feller,'

'And I'm the only one that can maybe keep it from happening.'

'Sure.'

He had to lower his head for a moment to relieve the pain, but forced it up again to rasp: 'I'll need help?'

'Reckon you could die if you moved that far, feller. Best I bring them to you in here?'

'I'd appreciate that, Steele.' He now stared unseeingly at the area of wall with the knot hole in it. Physical pain continued to mould the expression of his gaunt face beneath his totally hairless head, but a different brand of feeling sounded in his tone. 'And especially so because I guess it would suit your purpose better those kin of Avery Begley and the dude gunslinger were dead and gone? Along with me?'

'That wouldn't amount to being myself at all, feller,' Steele said tautly as he turned and went to the door.

'Especially for another reason, as well,' Orville Kyle pressed on, and when the Virginian met his dull-eyed gaze he thought that he could see dejected remorse in back of the predominant physical suffering. 'On account of you can't feel you owe anything to anyone in Rosarita? Me most of all? Way you were treated there?'

'Take another look at where that bullet went into you and be grateful you're such a mean bastard, sheriff.'

The lawman showed an expression that could have been a scowl or a soured grin as he rasped: 'You've lost me, Steele. But I can tell you one thing for sure: I don't have to look. I can feel this chunk of lead brewing up a mess of poison.'

'Right,' the Virginian responded as he stepped out of the doorway, but knew Kyle could still hear what he said as he moved off across the yard: 'So you know you'd be a dead man already if you were the big-hearted kind.'

11

Henry Bascomb, his drinker's nose not quite so purple after the long ride from town with its extra sobering experience of finding the corpse of the Nelson boy, pulled up short as he rounded the side of the house and saw the rifle-toting Virginian crossing the yard toward him. He was afraid for just a moment, before he recognised Steele and remembered what had been happening before the headlong, gun-blazing assault on the farmstead in the hollow.

'Oh, it's you! My, I guess we all just forgot about you what with all the excitement, Mr Steele. I saw you take the tumble off your horse. Are you all right? Not hurt? I'm going to bring the horses for the wagon and the buggy so we can——'

Matt Hope, whose horses the Begleys and Arness had rented, came hurrying around the corner, intent upon taking care of the chore for which he was obviously better suited.

'I'm in good shape, all things considered,' Steele answered, taking advantage of the pause that the liveryman's arrival forced upon the disconcerted doctor. 'But Kyle could use some of the attention you're best able to give, doc.'

'Orville Kyle?' Hope blurted.

Bascomb demanded to know: 'Where is the sheriff?'

'I'm in the barn, Henry!' the lawman tried to shout, but his tone was more a croak. 'If you have your bag of tricks with you, I'll be happy! But I need to talk to all you people before I . . . oh, shit, the bleeding's started again!'

121

The doctor rapped out an order to the liveryman that he should go bring his bag from his horse, then broke into a long, striding walk toward the doorway of the barn. The Virginian thought about emphasising Kyle's plea that Hope should also bring the rest of the Rosarita men and the new owners of the place: but decided it was unnecessary. So he took just a few moments to spot where his horse was contentedly cropping grass on the open range beyond the fallen-down fence, and then turned to go after Bascomb.

On his way into the barn he dragged one of the doors open wider for the expected crowd. And was ignored by the sheriff and the doctor as they engaged in a subdued argument: Bascomb attempting to be both placating and threatening in face of Kyle's croaking-voiced demands. A compromise was reached as Steele went to sit on a hay bale near the row of four stalls, only three of which were occupied by the rented horses. The agreement was reached on the basis that the gunshot man would be allowed to assume a seated posture with his back supported in the angle of the corner, provided the doctor could start his work at once.

It caused the big, bald-headed, haggard-looking lawman a great deal of pain as he was helped up into the attitude he wanted by the wiry little Bascomb, who kept making clucking noises of anxiety. Kyle pulled many faces, but managed to keep himself from crying out between his deep intakes of breath.

'I certainly hope you think that was all worthwhile,' the doctor said sourly. 'Because it may well have shortened your life by a considerable——'

Kyle looked up from peering at the wet fresh blood which had spilled out of the re-opened bullet hole to provide a bright contrast with that which had congealed. And said, as many footfalls were heard approaching the barn: 'Henry, a condemned man always has one last——'

'Let's see what kind of damage has been done to

122

you before we start talking death, Orville,' Bascomb snapped. And dropped to his knees beside Kyle so he was better able to unbutton the blood-sodden shirt.

The lawman looked to be drawing closer to total exhaustion by the moment. He also seemed to be on the point of throwing up. But then he shifted his pain-filled gaze from the doorway to fix it on Steele. And after a stretched second of intense concentration—like he was trying to remember who and where he was—he was able to overcome the heaviness of his drooping eyelids and to fight the acrid bile out of his rapidly working throat.

'You don't seem to be enjoying me going through this, mister?' he challenged as one shadow and then many fell across the doorway.

The Virginian inclined his head and replied: 'Maybe if I'd done it to you, feller?'

Then there was a whole barrage of questions asked and demands made as Matt Hope led the large group into the barn. Just the liveryman approached close to where Kyle sat and Bascomb eased the shirt away from the ugly bullet wound in the sheriff's near hairless chest: and after the bag was set down within reach of the doctor Hope scuttled back to become a part of the fifteen-strong gathering that had halted noisily on the threshold.

'Quiet!' the tall and thin, grey-haired and moustached Fraser Sorrel commanded, waving his arms in the air and stepping clear of the press of people. Half turned so that he could glare at them and direct quizzical glances toward Steele and the two men in the corner. 'Quieten it down and then maybe we'll find out what this is all about!'

He had a revolver in one of his gesturing hands. And most of the Rosarita men were carrying a handgun or a rifle. Which stressed the prisoner status of Arness and the Begley mother and son, the three of them close together at the front of the group. The older man

123

was as Steele had last seen him, but without the Winchester. Charlotte Begley was now wearing his suit jacket, cape fashion around her shoulders, with the lapels clutched tightly together at her throat. Dale, who seemed to be as recently out of bed as his mother, was hurriedly dressed in pants and shirt and boots that had not been laced. Fear had negated his arrogance and he looked shorter and thinner and paler than Steele remembered him from yesterday. And a great deal younger—a callow youth rather than a young man.

'I'm real grateful to you, Fraser,' Kyle rasped as the shocked group became subdued to such an extent that many of them held their breath. 'I'm in no shape to yell my head off to get heard.'

'What happened, Orville?' the owner of the Pioneer asked out of deep shock—more distraught than anyone else as he struggled to come to terms with this latest link in a chain of violence that had killed his son.

For a moment the wounded lawman came close to being sick to his stomach again as he stared into the helplessly bewildered face of Pierce Nelson's father. In this time, the fat little saloonkeeper shifted his gaze to look at Steele. And there was hostility in his tone and starting to reshape the expression on his face as he began:

'I told Michael Masterson and the Webb woman they was crazy to turn him loose without you bein' there to——'

'It wasn't Steele who plugged me, Dunc,' the lawman said quickly, before Nelson could complete the move of tracking his rifle to aim it at the abruptly tense Virginian. 'It was Pierce!'

There was a full second of stunned silence. Then an explosive burst of demands from many throats. That faltered and faded back into silence without anyone calling for quiet this time. And all eyes began to switch their gazes back and forth between Kyle and Nelson. Except for Bascomb, who continued to work on the lawman's bullet wound, using swabs and a strong-smelling liquid from his bag.

'Pierce is dead, Orville.'

'I know, Dunc. I killed him.'

The two statements were made in the same bald manner: and the utter tonelessness with which the men spoke set the pattern for what followed: with everyone remaining so icily calm that most sensed they were frozen into a dream sequence over which they had no control.

'Why'd you do that, Orville?'

'To keep him from killing me, Dunc.'

Bascomb interrupted his wound-cleansing chore and leaned back so that he could share a grim look between Kyle and Nelson. Then he swept an earnest gaze over every expectant bystander as he warned: 'Unless I get the opportunity to go in after the bullet pretty damn soon, the boy and the sheriff will have killed each other.'

'I need to say my piece, Henry.'

'Orville's decision, Henry,' Nelson added.

Bascomb sighed, shrugged and unfolded to his feet. 'Just so long as everyone knows I've expressed my opinion. Here, it's already infected, but we needn't take any more risks than we are already.'

He had stooped to delve into his bag again. Produced a wad of dressing which he placed in Kyle's good hand: then guided the hand so that the black hole encircled by a ridge of blue contusions was covered.

'Obliged,' the lawman said.

'And I'll be obliged if you'd get to how you and my boy came to——'

'Sure, Dunc. Everyone here—and back in town, I guess—deserves to know the whole story. And I'll tell it just like it happened. No excuses. And if anyone's feelings are hurt, to hell with them. Nobody's hurting more than me.'

He grimaced a lot of the time and occasionally drew

up the knees of his splayed legs. Frequently he had to swallow hard and every now and then needed to raise his damaged hand to support the left one in holding the dressing to the bullet wound. But he kept talking in the same toneless voice with which he had first admitted to killing the Nelson boy.

'Didn't feel right, letting those city folks come out here to take over from Avery without giving them more of a warning than they were ready to listen to in town. Came here and did just that. They heard me out this time. But Avery's woman and the boy and the city gunslinger with them made it plain to me they intended to stay and stand up against Lucas Hart. Since they have a right to what Avery left them, I figured I could do nothing more than warn them of the kind of trouble they'd likely bring down on themselves. And, like they rightly pointed out to me, as a peace officer it was my sworn duty to help them in protecting what was rightfully theirs.'

Dale Begley emphatically nodded, but a withering glare from his mother convinced him not to speak aloud his agreement.

'Thought then to ride on out to the Double-H and talk some turkey with Lucas Hart. But I never got anywhere near the house. Had a run in with Buck Ashton and Wylie at the trail line shack. Knew it was me but took a couple of shots at me anyway. Said they could have killed me if they had wanted and I knew they were speaking the truth. Told me every Double-H hand has instructions to run strangers off the spread. And far as Hart's concerned, anyone who doesn't work for him is a stranger. Anyone who objects is to be given a hard time. The way that scarfaced Irwin Wylie looked at me I got a pretty good idea of what was meant by hard time.

'Couldn't see there was anything else for me to do but head on back for town and warn folks to stay clear of the Double-H. Which was what I was doing when I met up with Pierce, Dunc. He was riding like there was a bunch of warpainted Apaches after him, and when he stopped he set to talking near as fast as he'd been riding. He was doing some crying in with the talking and I didn't understand too much of what he was blubbering. But I did get that he was planning on riding to the Double-H and asking Lucas Hart for a job.'

Now Duncan Nelson nodded, but it was less assertive than the Begley boy's earlier gesture had been and he felt no urge to back it with words. He pointedly avoided taking part in an exchange of knowing glances with Bascomb.

'I tried to talk Pierce out of what he planned,' Kyle continued in the same dispassionate tone after a pause for a gulp that perhaps sucked another threat of nausea from out of his throat. 'Started to tell him what happened to me with Ashton and Wylie. But he wouldn't listen. Told me he was through with me and everyone else in Rosarita. Including you, Dunc. Ordered me to move out of his way. When I tried to take a hold of the bridle of his gelding he pulled a gun out from under the duster he was wearing. He said afterwards it was a mistake. He hadn't meant to fire at me. The gun just went off.

'I fell off my horse and I thought I was going to die right there and then. Pierce backed his horse off and started to yell at me that it was my own fault. And your fault, Dunc. That nobody ever let him do what he wanted. He was ranting and raving and saying crazy things. Scared more than anything, I figure now. Then, I was just sure he wanted to kill me. And it was a crazy kid who was going to make me cash in my chips. Felt the need to take Pierce with me, Dunc. Never was that close to dying before, way I saw it. Just couldn't keep myself from drawing my gun and killing Pierce for what he was doing to me.

'He took off. I don't know if he was riding his horse or if the horse was in a bolt. Didn't even know if I'd hit him. After I'd stayed down on the trail for awhile I figured I wasn't about to die there and then. Was able to get up and remount my horse. And I headed on back to town. Found where Pierce had taken a fall off his gelding and was stretched out in the brush. I stayed there with him when I saw he was still alive. He asked me not to move him because the bullet in his belly didn't hurt him so much while he was down there in the brush the way he was. That's when he told me he hadn't meant to shoot me. Said a few other things, too. Amounted to that he was sorry for what had happened. To me. And that he'd been such a disappointment to you, Dunc. Then he died.'

Kyle was not through, but needed to take the time to concentrate his attention on not submitting to the compulsion to cry out as a wave of physical pain threatened to undermine his struggle to remain icily calm.

Nelson hung his head, gripped his rifle in white-knuckled fists and filled the pause with a strangled: 'Oh, God.'

'I didn't think I could make it to town. I'd lost a lot of blood and this bullet inside me felt like it was making poison faster than I could make spit to chew tobacco. Had it in mind to tie Pierce to his gelding before I set the horse to running for home, but I didn't have the strength. So I just set the horse to running. Then headed back for the Double-H. I still thought I was ready to cash in every step of the way and I guess I was off my head some, the way Pierce was. But the way it seemed, Lucas Hart was the one responsible for the mess I was in and I figured to call the bluff of Ashton or whoever else I might have run up against getting on to the Double-H. I already had one bullet in me. Get to see Hart and have it out with him, one way or the other. Prove I'm as good a lawman as Rosarita folks always thought I was.

'Never made it. Reached the spur that comes out to this place and knew I'd never make it all the way to the

Double-H. Not without some rest and some patching up. Planned to get that with the new people. I passed out someplace in the trees. Not for long, I guess. When I came out of it I was flat on my back on the trail and my horse was gone. Reached the house on foot. But wasn't anybody home and the place was locked up. Made for the barn here and curled up in this corner. Maybe to die. Maybe not. Slept like a dead man, until I heard Steele and the city folks talking. Then the shooting. That's it, Dunc. That's how Pierce and me came to shoot each other.'

The saloonkeeper did not have to take time to examine his feelings after Kyle had finished his monotone explanation. For he had been only half listening or not listening at all to what the sheriff said after the manner of his son's dying was recounted. And an expression of melancholy had gradually taken a firmer hold on his fleshy face.

'All through?' Bascomb asked, looking quickly between Nelson and Kyle as he squatted again beside the wounded man. 'Can I make an overdue full examination of the patient now?'

'I'm through,' the lawman answered and now that he had spoken his piece he looked greyer and gaunter and much older: as if the powerful need to tell of the tragedy had sustained his strength.

'It's usual for a doctor to treat a case in private,' Bascomb growled, with a critical glance that raked across all the bystanders.

But a mass move to comply with the request was checked when Duncan Nelson said morosely:

'My fault as much as anybody else's. Ever since his Ma died so young and him so young, I acted more like a mother than a father to him. Babied him and bawled him out when he kicked against it. Always told me he'd run off one day if I didn't give him no freedom. Last night when Henry and me got drunk in the Pioneer and——'

'No sense in trying to undo what's done, Dunc,' Bascomb advised earnestly.

'Well, I drove him away,' the saloonkeeper went on, ignoring the interruption. 'What with them hard-nosed Hart men sittin' out the funeral in the Pioneer and then the dude gunslinger showin' up in town. Filled Pierce's head with nonsense. When me and Henry were full of liquor, I told Pierce I'd take down his pants and paddle his bare ass if he didn't do like I wanted and cook us up a mess of supper. Made him feel small. And look it in front of Henry. He done what he was told, but later he upped and left town. My fault the next time I saw him, he was dead under a blanket.'

'A blanket?' Kyle queried, and now his voice sounded as exhausted as he looked.

'I guess the stranger?' Fraser Sorrel suggested with a quizzical glance at Adam Steele who had risen from the hay bale.

'Knew you Rosarita people were on my back trail and would do the rest of what's necessary,' the Virginian said.

'Later than was planned,' the stage and telegraph office man answered. 'Persuaded by some of the women to wait awhile longer for the sheriff to return.'

'I'm obliged you covered the body, mister,' Nelson said dully, gazing into the wretched middle distance instead of at Steele. 'Sent James Bate and his boy back to town with the body. Old man Cooper will be doing what's necessary by now, I figure.'

'Any reason we can't be startin' back to Rosarita now?' Matt Hope asked of anyone who cared to respond.

'Doc?' Sorrel asked, re-assuming his role as top hand among the townspeople now that they were no longer vengeance-bent vigilantes.

Bascomb ended his close-up examination of the bullet wound and dropped his magnifying glass in his bag. Stood up from the lawman who was breathing

130

shallowly but in all other respects looked dead. 'Orville's going to die if I don't dig the bullet out of him. The ride to town is going to shorten the odds on him pulling through. But he'd have no better chance if I did my surgery here without the proper facilities.'

'So we'll be getting back, all right, Dunc?' Sorrel suggested.

Nelson nodded absently, still almost lost in a black world of remorse.

'Best Orville rides back on that flatbed I saw out front,' Bascomb said.

'I'll hitch up the horses,' Matt Hope volunteered eagerly.

'Hey, we rented and paid——' Dale Begley began.

'Now, son, let's be charitable toward——' his mother attempted to placate.

The incensed youngster jerked his arm free of her reaching hand and snarled: 'Charitable, hell! They come out here to our place and shoot at us like . . . like I don't know what! Then they accuse us of murder! And it's my opinion they'd have lynched us if they didn't find out it was one of their own who murdered——'

'Leave it, Dale,' Fletcher Arness warned, softly but insistently out of the side of his mouth.

And the partially dressed young man felt compelled to end his tirade as he immediately became aware of the dangerous mixture of contempt and menacing hostility with which he was being eyed by the Rosarita men. But it was the approach of the impassive-faced Steele that caused him to step back and to the side—and perhaps it was not his intention that he should move into the protective embrace of his mother. Although he made no attempt to break away from her this time.

'You fired the first shot, kid,' the Virginian reminded the apprehensive young man as he made for the gap in the group on the barn threshold left by Begley's retreat.

131

'But I thought it was all a trick and——'

'So you made a mistake, Dale,' Arness pointed out, as stone faced as the Virginian.

'Yeah. That's right. It was a mistake!'

'Same as Pierce gettin' killed was,' the grieving father said dully. 'Mistakes get made all the time.'

'Some do, sure enough,' Steele drawled as he directed an ice-eyed sidelong glance at the youngster cowering in the curled arm of his mother. 'Others are born.'

12

The big black stallion allowed himself to be captured without the least protest by the man who had forced him into a potentially dangerous fall no more than a half hour ago. Then stood patiently and with not the least show of rancour while the man ran his expert eye and a gloved hand over every part of him that could have been damaged by the fall.

Which attitude by his mount caused Adam Steele to feel humbled as he swung up astride the saddle and heeled the horse into an easy walk that headed him up out of the hollow at the rear of the farmstead. But at the same time as he experienced this not entirely un-familiar sense of humility because of the disposition of a horse, he also felt a sharpening of his determination to get into the stud business. To work with, and so be in almost exclusive contact with, dumb animals; which although they could be ornery and mean, did not carry grudges. For the most part were of a forgiving and forgetting nature, from which a man of perception who was so inclined could easily learn.

From the rim of the hollow where the pastureland was featured with rock outcrops and through which a path of churned-up ground had been laid by the recent stampede, Steele reined in his mount and looked back down at the farmstead below. For a second or so expressed a grimace as he reflected on how he had felt the compulsion to take revenge upon the hapless Dale Begley for almost killing him. This after any notion of causing Kyle to pay for the beating and imprisonment was thwarted by the bullet he had taken in the chest.

He had felt additionally frustrated by the certainty that, much as he would have liked the opportunity to give horse ranching a try in this part of the country, it was not to be.

But at least, he concluded with an almost imperceptible sigh that bridged the gap between the grimace and his customary impassiveness, he had been able to confine the venting of his bad feeling to a cheap crack at the kid. But as he now acknowledged this fact and prepared to indulge himself in another period of contentment, the stallion nickered and tossed his head. And the Virginian felt it necessary to run a gloved hand down the side of the animal's neck and admit aloud:

'You're right. Even that was wrong. You didn't even give me the evil eye for upending you the way I did.'

Now the animal vented a terse snort and through smiling teeth Steele rasped in a good-natured tone: 'Enough, feller. One of the reasons I like horses so much is that I don't have to get into conversation with them.'

This time there was no response by sound or gesture from the stallion. He just stood among the scattering of rocks that jutted up at many angles out of the lush grass on the ridge, patiently waiting for the command to move. Which was something Steele found he was strangely reluctant to give. Because from the rim of the hollow he was able to get a panoramic view across the country in every direction. Vistas of rolling hills carpeted with verdant grass for as far as distant mountain ranges or extensive timber stands or the shimmering heat haze of noon allowed the eye to see. With, here and there, small patches of trees or clumps of brush and outcrops or unobtrusive escarpments of rock to add visual interest of varied shape and colour. Close by there was the small lake that at present was fenced off because it had been poisoned. To the north and the east there were other small bodies of water glinting in the light of the midday sun. And a couple of creeks further supplied this fine piece of country with the pure water that nurtured its greenness between rains.

Perhaps two miles to the east, along the top of a rise, a length of fencing emerged from one stand of timber and was in view for something over a thousand feet before the strands of wire were carried out of sight on the downslope beyond the hill crest. Apart from the barrier that encircled the poisoned fishing pool closer by, the distant fence that obviously formed the boundary line between the Double-H spread and Begley land was the only sign of man's encroachment on nature that was visible from this spot—unless the Virginian looked down into the hollow. Which he did now, his eye seemingly drawn to track the route of the stampede toward the gap forced through the rear section of the fence enclosing the cultivated patch of rich land.

His attention was attracted by a brief burst of vocal sound: the voices muted by distance but the tone distinctly ill-humoured. The men from Rosarita were leaving to return to town. All but for three of them mounted on the horses they had ridden here. Orville Kyle was under some blankets in the back of the flatbed, Doc Bascomb crouched beside him, and Matt Hope driving the rig. The two spare saddle horses were hitched on at the rear. The heated exchange was quickly drowned out by the thud of many hooves against hard-packed dirt and then came to an end soon afterwards—nobody riding horseback or aboard the wagon gave more than a passing backward glance toward Fletcher Arness and the Begley mother and son who stood in the front yard beside the carelessly parked cut-under buggy. Next, before the departing townspeople had gone more than a couple of hundred feet toward the timber on the southern rim of the hollow, the trio swung around and strode out of Steele's field of vision to go into the house.

It would not have been his choice to live here, he mused as he continued to sit his saddle on the horse among the outcrops. During his ride from the property marker where the trail cut across the boundary line he had seen a dozen places where a house would be better sited. And, he realised suddenly, he was lingering on one such spot now: disinclined to ride away from the Begley place as he envisaged building a house on this rim of the hollow. Maybe working the fields down there in back of the old Begley house, and keeping hogs and chickens and a milk cow to supply the table. But a man did not live by food alone. If he had discovered nothing else during the long and violent years since he rode away from the Steele plantation to go to war, he had learned the truth of that old saw. A man could exist, he could endure, he could make the best of what life allowed him: but he could not truly live a life in which the sole purpose was to stay alive. He had to strive toward and attain something more. In the case of Adam Steele, something similar to what he had left behind in Virginia—something like a home in this idyllic setting with a herd of free-running thoroughbred horses to put to good use the fine pasturelands that had been allowed to go to waste for so long by the eccentric Avery Begley.

Though who was he to call the tragic, newly-dead man an eccentric, the Virginian acknowledged with a wry smile that was self-denigrating. Begley had been a man who had lost everything he believed in and everyone he loved. Then he had head off into the unknown, to return with enough money and determination to buy a large enough piece of land to ensure his peace of mind. And to remain there, leading the kind of life he had chosen, until his weak constitution was finally allied with the tactics of attrition employed by a powerful neighbour, and he had to be carried off his place, soon to breathe his last. There were several parallels to be drawn with the past life and future aims of Adam Steele—although he did not envisage a similar ending. As far as he knew, his heart was sound. And he had a wealth of experience to draw on to guide his dealings with a man like Lucas Hart and the kind of hard-nosed help the rancher hired.

He pursed his lips, with the intention of venting a soft sigh and a command to his mount. Instead, he directed a globule of saliva to the side that he had been preparing to turn the stallion. And tugged the reins in the opposite direction as he gently heeled the animal back down into the hollow. The expression on his heavily-bristled, slightly sweat-beaded face had more in common with the spit at the ground than the composed manner in which he set the horse into motion.

Sheriff Orville Kyle was right. Charlotte Begley and her son were entirely unsuitable to run this place: albeit with the equally citified Fletcher Arness to help them deal with Lucas Hart and his men. Steele had not yet had a proper opportunity to put a proposition to the Begleys: and unless he made one last try to talk business with them in a calm and collected manner he was sure he would regret this for evermore as a lost opportunity.

'Yeah, I know,' he murmured softly to his well schooled mount that had complied without protest to the command to head back down into the hollow. But now pricked his ears to the sound of the voice. 'I need to have my brains tested. But I don't reckon there's a light bright enough to shine that far up my ass.'

13

It was very quiet down in the bottom of the hollow again now that the Rosarita men had ridden into the timber. And, just as when Steele had first approached the house on the track between the overgrown fields, so now as he closed with it from the rear the only sign of life within the dilapidated building was the smoke rising from the chimney.

He thought he could detect an appetising aroma of frying meat intermingled with the acrid taint of burning wood. And as he rode slowly around the front corner of the barn and reined in his mount at the side of the back yard his mind was filled with the tantalising image of sharing a home-cooked meal with the easy-on-the eye Charlotte Begley while they discussed the details of a deal. The woman having commanded her snotty son and her swaggering protector to remain silently in the background while she listened with high interest to how a partnership could work. She and Dale and Fletcher Arness would have to return to the city from whence they had come, of course. And Steele would require first refusal to purchase the property if ever a sale was to be contemplated. For his part, the Virginian would put the land to good use raising blood-stock horseflesh and would see that it was kept in fine order—which included dealing with the trouble caused by the Double-H owner or anybody else.

Of course, such a scheme assumed that the Begleys had no firm plans of their own for their inheritance . . . And probably assumed a whole lot of other things, Steele allowed with a fleeting grimace as he swung

138

down out of the saddle and eyed the windowless rear wall of the house. It was not in his nature to extend his thought processes so far in advance based upon such unknowns and unpredictables. But, damnit, he had been doing much of late that was uncharacteristic of him. Which had to be a measure, he reflected ruefully, of just how intently he was getting to desire the fulfilment of his ambition.

Hoofbeats of a bunch of horses at the gallop sounded in the distance and for perhaps a full two seconds he had the impression that he heard this only in imagination: and he almost conjured up a picture of a herd of saddleless and unbridled thoroughbreds fired to race across the open range for no other reason than the simple joy of living free on such beautiful land.

But then a woman shouted: 'Fletcher, riders coming!'

And the quiet smile of pleasure that had begun to spread across Steele's face was gone in an instant. And a grimace of malcontent was back in the line of his mouth and the coldness of his black eyes. This as he led his horse toward the entrance of the barn where one of the double doors still stood wide open from when the Rosarita men had crowded onto the threshold with their prisoners to listen to Kyle talk them out of a possible lynching. Now, after he and the stallion were inside the barn, Steele dragged the door almost closed again. One of the hinges protested rustily, but the creaking sound would not have carried far against the rising volume of hoofbeats at the gallop. The movement of the door could have been seen though: by the frontrunners of the bunch of men who plunged their mounts out of the trees and through the gateless entrance to start down into the hollow.

Nine or ten men, most of them obscured to a greater or lesser extent by the billowing dust of the gallop. But as they drew closer to the house, so they slowed their pace: and over lessening distance with a less dense cloud of dust to contend with, Steele was able to recognise the curly-haired Buck Ashton as one of the two men at the head of the column. The scar-faced Irwin Wylie was in the bunch, also. And he didn't doubt that Rex Lowry and Marv Ritter had come calling on the new owners of the place, too. But there was little time to attempt more than a cursory survey of the riders before they dropped down into the hollow low enough to be lost to his sight by the intervening bulk of the house. And for most of the final few seconds when the frontrunners were still in view he concentrated on the man riding to the left of Ashton.

A silver-haired man with a face stained dark brown by the elements, the skin that was stretched over the sparse flesh and prominent bone structure looking to be heavily and deeply lined. Not a young man. Not tall or with a powerful build. But there was something in the way he sat his horse that suggested he was a man who possessed a commanding presence, and Steele guessed this was Lucas Hart himself. He was dressed in much the same style as the younger men—in the working cowpuncher's garb such as his top hand and the other three had worn yesterday as they sat out the funeral in the Pioneer.

The Virginian went to his horse to slide the Colt Hartford out of the boot, then left the animal to wander at will in the sunlit barn that was redolent with equine smells that did not quite yet mask the more pungent taint of the lotion Doc Bascomb had used to clean the sheriff's bullet wound. And sweated more heavily as he returned to the cracked open door. Was aware, perhaps only in his imagination, of some old pains starting to hurt a little. He could no longer detect the fragrance of frying meat in with the wood smoke that still rose in a straight column from the chimney at one end of the house.

For a while he listened to the many sounds made by many men reining in their mounts after a lengthy

140

gallop. And he did not concentrate upon trying to hear anything else until there was just an occasional animal snort, human spit and a combination of heavy breathing from out front of the house. Was tensed, in particular, to hear if any Double-H man was coming out back to check on the barn.

'What the hell do you people want?' Dale Begley snarled suddenly.

'Tell you what we don't want,' came the answer, and Steele recognised the voice of the blond, good looking Marv Ritter. 'We don't want no lip from some sassy kid who ain't near old enough to have stopped a-suckin' on his Moma's titty.'

'Why, you——'

'Shut up, Dale!' Arness snapped to cut in on the youngster's shrill anger.

But it was apparently not sufficient to check his rage at the insult. And there was the sharp crack of an open-handed blow on bare flesh. Dale's shriek was pitched higher than his voice had been. Then this venting of pain was cut short by his mother as she warned in an ice cold tone:

'One day you'll learn to do as you're told by those who know best, son.'

There was a pause of a second or so before the owner of the Double-H spread said: 'My apologies for the uncouthness of my help, Mrs Begley. I guess most of my men are not too familiar with the genteel ways of city folks like you. But, by the same token, I would have expected folks such as you to open your door to visitors making a neighbourly call.'

'There!' the woman answered, sounding less cold. And the way she flung open the door so that it slammed violently against the inside wall emphasised the strain she was under to keep control of her anger. 'And it's *Miss* Begley. Avery and I never married.'

'That kinda makes the kid a bastard, I guess?' either the scar-faced Wylie or Rex Lowry taunted.

Then followed a sudden upsurge of sound that caused Steele to tense for the expected climax—as many men drew and cocked their guns. But Lucas Hart barked:

'Hold it, boys!' Then he moderated his tone to add: 'Let's do our best to keep this polite, uh?'

'Miss Begley and I didn't exactly have the welcome mat put out for us when we tried to call on you last night, sir,' Fletcher Arness said, and sounded firmly in control of himself.

'*Touché*,' the rancher allowed, and pronounced it impeccably. But then he over-emphasised his south-western accent as he went on: 'Like you city folks say. But we folks out here in the sticks, we're the early to bed, early to rise kind. Except for those that hire on to see a man's property and belongings are protected.'

As Steele eased the door open a little further, the rusty hinge hardly making itself heard, he recalled what Orville Kyle had said about the newcomers to the Begley place being out when he came back here to rest up in the middle of the night after the Nelson boy shot him.

'Dale was a stupid fool to go out to the Double-H the way he did at the time he did,' Arness admitted. 'But the men who stopped him knew who he was. Just as they knew who we were when we got there before they could do the boy serious harm.'

'They wouldn't have——'

There was the crack of another open-handed blow that caused the youngster to cry out again. His mother warned him tautly:

'You've been told to hold your tongue!'

'The boy sounds like he could have been spoilt in the past, Mrs . . . Miss Begley,' Hart said conversationally as Steele slid out of the barn doorway and moved between the hog pen and the chicken run, heading for the firmly closed rear door of the house. 'Reaping the error of your early ways now.'

142

'I'd be appreciative if you would get to the point of your visit here, Mr Hart,' the woman said as Steele pressed his back to the wall on the hinged side of the door, the Colt Hartford angled diagonally across the front of his body in tight fists.

'I was about to remark that you are now showing wisdom in the way you chastise your son, Miss Begley.' This close to the door, Steele heard muted whispers from inside the house. Visualised the youngster rasping a curse at the rancher and his mother hushing him up with a dire warning. 'And to say I trust you may be as wise in accepting the offer I intend to make to you.'

'To buy us out?' Arness asked.

'I am given to understand that the late lamented Avery Begley left this property to his wife,' Hart countered in a dismissive tone.

'Guess his bastard son maybe has a say in——' one of the Hart hands started.

'Listen you bunch of smart aleck knowalls!' Charlotte Begley snarled and Steele heard her heavy footfalls as she stomped out over the threshold at the front of the house. And although she had now abandoned her attempt to remain coldly aloof to the unwelcome visitors she was able to hold her temper on a tight rein.

'Charlotte!' Fletcher Arness rasped anxiously.

'Mother!' Dale yelled, in greater fear.

She ignored both pleas to hurl her contemptuous admonition at Hart and his men. 'I was married for more than two years before Dale was born! His father——'

'Lady, we're not concerned with none of that,' Wylie broke in. 'Right, Mr Hart?'

'What's over and done with is over and done with,' the rancher said. 'Whether it happened all those years ago. Or just last night.'

With his mother well beyond arm's reach out front of the house, Dale felt secure enough from punishment to

143

snarl: 'I went out there to tell you not to bother trying to scare us off, big shot!'

'My men told me that, son. And my men don't lie to me,' Hart acknowledged evenly. 'Miss Begley, Mr Arness . . . They also told me you apologised for the boy's crass behaviour in trying to invade my privacy at such an ungodly hour. Then you told my men much the same thing as the boy had said. But in a more civil manner. You are unprepared to entertain any kind of offer for the property you have inherited?'

'That's about what happened and what was said,' Arness allowed and it sounded to Steele as if the man had now stepped outside to be with Charlotte Begley.

'It was not our intention to put it so bluntly,' the woman augmented. 'But since your men were on the point of flogging my son my temper became somewhat frayed.'

'I was told the boy needed to be restrained.'

'Damn right I did.'

The woman made a sound of irritated impatience. Then pointed out: 'You are right, Mr Hart. It is over and done with. It was a stupid and unseemly disturbance in the middle of the night. But as far as we are concerned, it served a useful purpose. Or should have done. You know we have no intention of selling the Begley ranch to you. Nor, I should perhaps add, to anyone else.'

For a stretched second the Virginian had the notion his return to the place had been seen and Charlotte Begley knew he was close enough to be eavesdropping on the exchange.

'But apparently it was not made plain enough to you?' she went on. 'Or you and your bully boys would not be here now?'

'I have a great deal of trust in my men when they are doing my bidding, ma'am,' Hart replied. 'I have never instructed them to negotiate property purchases on my behalf. I am here now to offer you——'

144

'A million dollars——'

'Do not be ridiculous, Miss Begley,' Hart snapped.

'If you had let me finish,' the woman snapped back, 'you would have heard me say a million dollars would not be enough to buy one square foot of this land you killed Avery to get!'

'Careful, lady,' Buck Ashton advised icily.

'That's all right, my friend,' the rancher said, but there was a tautness in his tone that suggested it required an effort by him to say this. But Steele was sure he expended a far greater quantity of nervous energy as he reached for the handle of the door, turned it a fraction of an inch at a time and then began to ease it inwards as soon as he felt the tongue had been withdrawn out of the recess. This as Lucas Hart was saying: 'These people are strangers hereabouts and maybe they've heard some unfounded rumours.' He hardened his tone then, as he went on: 'But let me tell you, Miss Begley, Mr Arness and you, boy—my men don't lie to me and I lie to no one. I nor anybody working for me killed Avery Begley. I will admit that I made it difficult for him to live here as my neighbour. But it was never my intention he should die.'

Steele had eased the door open wide enough so that he could swing away from the wall in an arcing about-face, so that he was able to peer with one eye through the crack between the door's edge and the jamb. As he completed the silent move he took a double-handed grip on the uncocked Colt Hartford again: the rifle angled so he could use the muzzle as a ram to thrust the door wide.

'No matter what you intended, he's under six feet of earth in the Rosarita cemetery now, Mr Hart,' Charlotte Begley accused in a toneless voice. And she could not have directed a greater weight of contemptuous reproach at the rancher had she shrieked the accusation at the top of her voice.

Steele could not see Dale within his restricted field

of vision across the spartanly furnished room. But he could hear heavy, frightened breathing from somewhere over to the right. And he guessed the boy was at the window he had shattered with a gunshot earlier. What the Virginian was able to see across a pine table and the top of a chair back was the wide open front doorway and a section of the yard beyond. Where, some six feet away from the threshold, Charlotte Begley and Fletcher Arness stood shoulder to shoulder, facing the Double-H hands, who remained in their saddles. But the men were no longer in a double-file column. They had moved into a tight-knit group, with the commanding figure of Hart and the curly-haired Ashton beside him still at the centre front. Within the confined view through the door frame Steele could see five other men. The scar-faced Wylie who was smoking a cigar: the others unknown to him. If any of these men had drawn a revolver from his holster or a rifle from his boot at the outset of the confrontation, all their guns had since been put up.

'That cannot be denied,' Hart responded to the woman's charge with a slight inclination of his head. Now that he had a closer and clearer view of the man, the Virginian thought the rancher was older than he had seemed at first sight. Perhaps was even a well-preserved seventy. 'And it takes us into the realms of what has been done and how it cannot be undone. We must concern ourselves with what remains to be achieved. Or wasted.'

'That sounds like a threat?' Arness muttered.

'The lady has said her last word on the subject of what she intends to do with this property?' Hart countered.

'I intend to live here,' Charlotte Begley told him resolutely.

Hart inclined his head again and said evenly as he backed his horse out from the centre of the group: 'I wasted a great deal of time with the previous owner and

146

time is something a man of my advanced years cannot afford to waste. So I do not propose to squander very much more in the pursuit of this particular aspiration of mine.'

'Is that your last word, or is it a threat, Mr Hart?' Arness asked, and stepped protectively in front of the woman.

The rancher checked the backward movement of his mount, and his face that had been hard set now expressed sadness as he answered: 'To you, mister, my last word is goodbye.'

Irwin Wylie was fast on the draw, but one of the other men hidden to Steele's narrow-eyed gaze was faster. Unless he already had his gun clear of the holster. Whichever, the out of sight man shot first—as the woman vented a strangled cry of shock and Steele started to thrust open the door with the muzzle of the Colt Hartford.

On the periphery of his vision the Virginian saw Dale swing away from the window, the boy's expression a match for the emotion that had sounded in his mother's scream: this as the centre of his attention was held by the spurt of gunsmoke with a streak of flame at its tail that exploded with a bullet from the barrel of Wylie's revolver.

Then Fletcher Arness started to go down, executing a half turn away from the position he had taken as a shield in front of the woman. Both his hands clutched at the area on the left side of his chest from which blood was spurting. There was a less forceful eruption of bright crimson from the hole above his left eye into which the second bullet had tunneled. He was rigidly dead as he began the fall, then collapsed into a limp heap on the sun-bright yard as his muscles gave a final spasm and surrendered their functions.

For a fraction of a second Charlotte Begley and Adam Steele were held in frozen attitudes. She in a state of debilitating horror as she stared down at the

147

dead man. The Virginian locked in a forward-striding action as he gazed at Dale Begley: unable to move as he recognised with a blinding flash of reason that he was a stretched second away from getting himself killed. And killed for no good reason. Killed because he had reacted with reckless instinctiveness to the brutal gunning down of an unarmed man. A man who, if he was anything to him, was his enemy. In terms of him being allied with Charlotte Begley in her determination not to sell her inheritance.

The scar-faced Wylie had cocked his revolver again by then. And exposed his teeth in an eager grin—teeth that were slightly parted so that they gripped without biting off the end of his wispily smoking cigar. Grin, cigar and handgun were all aimed through the front doorway of the house, across the table and chair back and at the unmoving Virginian who was framed on the rear threshold.

Now Steele moved the gloved thumb of his left hand, to pull back the hammer of the Colt Hartford. The sound made by the cocking action of the rifle was masked by the thud of Dale Begley's footfall as the boy came far enough across the room to reach for the Winchester that Arness had left leaning against the side of the pine table.

'I'll kill you, boy!' the Virginian roared with such power that his voice seemed to fill the tiny house and explode out of the shattered windows and open doorways with a tangible force.

It acted to freeze the youngster while his clawed hands were still several inches short of getting a grip on the leaning Winchester. And in the moments of utter silence that followed the bellowed threat, Steele sensed many more eyes than those of the grinning Wylie and the perplexed Dale Begley fastened upon him.

'You . . ?' the boy croaked.

'Why?' his mother managed to vent from her shock-constricted throat.

'You bast—' the youngster started, and leaned far enough forward to get a hand on the Winchester.

But Steele plunged into fluid movement, too. Leapt off the threshold rather than took a stride toward the snarling boy. Half turned from the waist and swung the rifle into a fuller turn. So that the muzzle raked away from its aim at Dale Begley. But the side of the rosewood stock made vicious contact with the side of the boy's head. Knocked him out on his feet and sent him sprawling across the floor like he was a loosely-packed sack of feed.

His mother lunged away from the dead Arness and flung herself down on to her haunches beside him as he came to rest on the threshold of the front door. And Steele was careful to keep the Colt Hartford aimed at the floor as he replied to her query:

'Things aren't always how they seem, ma'am.'

'I can believe what I see with my own eyes!' she challenged as she sank forward on to her knees and held the blood-leaking head of her son against the slope of her thighs; pushed out one of her hands that was stained red.

'Don't they say you sometimes have to be cruel to be kind?' Steele drawled as he advanced slowly across the room.

'Hell, we can see you're all heart,' Irwin Wylie growled sardonically and then a hollow laugh exploded from between his clenched teeth. Which he ended abruptly to add: 'You must have one big as Texas, I figure.'

Steel came to a halt at the doorway that was blocked by the unconscious boy and his kneeling mother, swept his cold-eyed gaze over all the mounted men and drawled: 'For a while there, I reckon I had a head that was about as empty.'

14

As Duncan Nelson failed to respond to the Virginian's quizzical double-take at the silver star pinned to the shirt front of the saloonkeeper, Buck Ashton said:

'It's the guy I told you about, Mr Hart. The one who hit town just as they were planting Avery Begley.'

Nelson was pretending he needed to look intently at what he was doing as he pushed a Winchester back into his saddle boot. And now Steele raked his gaze away from the only Rosarita man in the group to give his full attention to the elderly rancher. Who had eyes as coal black as his own. Then Hart displayed his ability to drain his dark eyes of every trace of emotion after he gave a nod of acknowledgement that ended the level stare of deep and blatantly unconcealed interest he had been directing at the coldly impassive Virginian.

'Deputy Nelson said you'd left, Mr Steele?'

'I thought he'd left,' the Virginian replied, disconcertingly aware of how the woman at his feet was staring up at him in distraught bewilderment as she cradled her son's bloodied head. 'I also thought he was in the saloon business.'

'I am——' Nelson started.

'I understand you plan on getting into the horse raising business?' Hart said to summarily block out the other man.

'Soon as I can find the right piece of land.'

'My advice is that you should look for a suitable property in another part of the country, Mr Steele.'

'Arizona certainly doesn't appear to be as healthy as I've heard, feller. For men who don't take your advice, anyway.'

Steele inclined his head toward the spread-eagled corpse of Fletcher Arness. And some of the Double-H men moved toward drawing weapons. But Hart caused them to check what they were doing—much to the relief of Duncan Nelson—when he snapped:

'Easy boys.' Then moderated his tone to ask of Steele: 'Guess you heard what I said about Avery Begley passing away?'

'Before that I heard that no laws were broken.'

The silver-haired, gnarled-skinned rancher inclined his head. 'And no law has been broken here this afternoon, Mr Steele.'

'Just because some beer seller puts on a lawman's badge?' Charlotte Begley rasped, swinging her head around to glare malevolently at Hart. 'That doesn't make cold-blooded murder anything else but what it is!'

The high emotion died as she looked fleetingly at the corpse before she bent over her raggedly breathing son: and splashed his blood-run face with the tears of silent weeping.

'Like both of you people know, the Rosarita sheriff is indisposed,' Hart went on with his explanation as if there had been no bitter interjection. 'The boys and me ran into Kyle and the rest of the townspeople at the start of the spur to this place. The same time we met up, young Leroy Bate from the town grocery store came hell for leather along the trail. With a telegraph in answer to one that Kyle sent last afternoon. Seems the name of Fletcher Arness started ringing bells in the back of the sheriff's mind. From when he was a lawman in another part of the country. And the bells weren't ringing for nothing. Telegraph that came in on the wire this morning confirmed that man's wanted for a killing in Wichita.'

'Right enough,' Nelson insisted on putting in. 'Orville got the telegraph and it was brought out by the Bate boy. Orville bein' so badly shot up, he deputised me to——'

151

'That was fifteen years ago,' the woman sobbed. 'And it was self-defence!'

'Time don't make no difference, lady,' Nelson argued. 'And since that there Arness went on the run from town before he could get arrested and tried, I guess there ain't any way he can claim self——'

'There's no way on earth he can claim anything now, feller,' Steele cut in.

'That sure is true enough,' Lucas Hart allowed, and now backed his horse off far enough so he was able to wheel him clear of the group of Double-H hands and the saloonkeeper from town. But he held the animal on a tight rein as he looked over his shoulder. 'But's what's done can't be undone, stranger. Was our intention for the deputy to arrest that Arness feller and arrange for him to be shipped up to Wichita. Just didn't work out easy as that, did it?'

'Because you——' the woman attempted to accuse.

'We can all see that he's empty-handed now,' Hart went on insistently. 'But I guess there isn't a man here, including a duly sworn in deputy sheriff, who'd deny he was certain Fletcher Arness—a wanted killer—was about to draw a weapon when he stepped in front of the lady?'

He glanced to left and right and inclined his head in acknowledgement of the muted chorus of affirmative sounds he drew with the implied query. Then he made to face away from the dilapidated house that had been further ravaged by a barrage of bullets. And his men and Nelson made to wheel their horses. But the sight of Charlotte Begley rising to her feet caused all of them to check their departure.

'Get off my land, you double-dealing, four-flushing, murdering swine,' she snarled in low-toned vehemence. 'And be warned. If I see any one of you or your kind on this property again, I'll——'

'You're overwrought, Miss Begley,' Buck Ashton cut in.

'Get the hell away from here, I told you,' she retorted, her voice rising and every semblance of good breeding had left her now.

'Ma'am, I came here in good faith to make you an offer,' Lucas Hart told her. 'This other matter is unfortunate. We can, of course, all be thankful that Steele intervened in the manner he did to prevent possible bloodshed by those who are innocent of anything but stupidity.'

'Mister, I——'

'But don't count on his help in the future if you should continue to refuse my offer to buy you out,' Hart snapped, his tone hardening. 'Unless he has led a blameless life?'

'You get Mr Hart's drift?' Wylie asked, and his eyes shifted their sardonically-smiling gaze between the woman and the Virginian.

'The telegraph's real fast, but it's a big country, uh?' Buck Ashton added, and there was unsmiling menace in his eyes as he met the impassive gaze of Steele for a stretched second.

The rancher was already moving his horse across the yard, past the buggy, toward the start of the track that cut between the overgrown fields on the southern side of the hollow. And now, as Steele needed to struggle to remain coldly impassive as a mask to the anger of bitter frustration, all the other riders formed into a column of two behind Hart. Then, within moments, their mounts were stirring up an elongated cloud of billowing dust as they were spurred into a gallop.

The motes were still settling on the yard and the parked buggy and the sprawled corpse when the sounds of the departure had been sufficiently diminished by distance for the woman's quiet voice to be clearly heard by Steele when she said:

'I'm in your debt, mister. They would surely have killed Dale if he had laid a hand on the rifle.'

'They could have claimed self-defence, I reckon.

And if they had let me live I wouldn't have been able to challenge them.'

She moved away from the prostrated form that breathed, to stand over the one that was utterly lifeless. As she ran the sleeve of the dress she now wore across her tear-moist eyes, Steele glanced around the one room that was all the house boasted. It was furnished with little more than the table and chair and the stove on which a pot of stew was no longer simmering because more fuel was needed in the grate. Somebody had slept in the single bed at the other end of the room last night. The other two on blankets on the floor.

'Fletcher killed a few men in his day, Mr Steele,' Charlotte Begley admitted to recapture his indifferent attention. 'All of them in self-defence. He claimed. Fact that he was paid to kill them, and called them out when he knew he was faster on the draw . . .'

She left the confession of culpability unfinished and when she looked up from the body and saw Steele emerging from the house, she gave a just discernible shrug.

'Reckon he hasn't done any gunslinging for a long time?'

She nodded. 'Since that killing in Wichita. Since then we've been taking care of each other the best way we've been able.'

'Sure.'

'Fletcher and I were brother and sister!' she said, angrily and defensively.

The Virginian, his own anger that had been aroused by the parting remarks of the Double-H men now reduced to an almost non-existent ball of ice at the pit of his stomach, found himself mildly surprised by the revelation.

'He was always the black sheep of the family,' the woman went on, the impulse to anger gone. And the strain of struggling to talk without betraying the depth of another brand of emotion was detectable only in

154

an occasional tremor of her voice. 'Even when we were much younger, on the farm in Maine where we grew up. We both came late to city life, Mr Steele. The Rosarita sheriff was wrong to think we know nothing about running a place such as this.'

She encompassed the hollow and the surrounding country with a weary gesture of a hand. Then sighed. 'But I expect we did encourage local people to think that way about us. The way we played up to them when it was obvious they had pre-judged us as . . . I truly was married for over two years before Dale came into the world, Mr Steele.'

'You don't have to tell me all this, lady,' the Virginian said as he peered up at the rim of the hollow over which the last of the Double-H men had ridden out of sight.

'His father was a gambler and a drunkard,' she pressed on as she looked in the same direction, her tone of voice insistent as she determined to set the record straight for her lone listener. 'But he was my legal husband when our son was conceived. And when he died with Dale just a baby I was left a widow. I was destitute and I had no idea where Fletcher was at the time. Only the Almighty knows what would have become of me and Dale had not Avery Begley taken care of us.

'He had just lost his wife and children and he needed the consolation I was able to offer him. He began to gamble, much as my husband did. But he wasn't a drinker. And he knew when to stop gambling. And he knew where to stop as far as I was concerned, Mr Steele. He treated me as a daughter, no more. Which was why I called myself Miss Begley when he was taking care of us. And after he left us I couldn't bring myself to change it back. To Arness or to the name of that . . . that man I was married to.

'He left us as suddenly as he came. Walked out of the house one evening and never returned. It was no great surprise. He was strange in a lot of ways. I heard rumours that he'd had a big win and I halfway believed them. He was always talking about striking it rich enough so he could buy a ranch and . . .' She gave another of the small shrugs and glanced disconsolately at the tumble-down house and weed-choked fields spreading up the slopes of the hollow. 'It seems he bought what he wanted, but didn't know what to do with it when he got it.'

'We all want different things out of life,' Steele said as they both looked at the doorway where Dale Begley was groaning back to consciousness.

'Even if I didn't plan on giving this place a better chance than Avery, I don't think you'd be interested in buying it anymore?' she asked as the Virginian turned to start toward the corner of the house.

He paused there to look back at her. 'It was a long time ago for me, too. But I can't even claim self-defence. So I reckon I've just got to keep moving on.' He tipped his hat with the gloved hand not holding the rifle against his shoulder and wished the woman: 'Good luck to you.'

'Had plenty of the other kind, Mr Steele,' she replied morosely as she shifted her gaze to the corpse and then started forward to help her son sit up in the house doorway. 'And the other kind is what other people are going to get plenty of if they try to make me regret I decided to . . .

. . . STOP HERE.'*

*Like this story. But Adam Steele will return in the near future to make THE SUNSET RIDE.